Declan Gallagher is from the town of Letterkenny in Co Donegal. He worked in the construction industry from an early age. He emigrated to London in the mid-eighties and then to New York, a year later, where he worked in a Mafia-controlled Concrete Union, then to Carpenter Union using false names provided by the construction companies.

During his time there, he became aware of the danger of working with these companies and how many Irish men were murdered for crossing the Mafia.

New York of today is a much safer place, and the Mafia no longer have the same control in the construction industry.

The Poisoned Glen tells the story of the influence this had on illegal Irish emigrants and how some met their untimely death.

I would like to dedicate this book to my late father,
Eamonn Gallagher.

Declan Gallagher

THE POISONED GLEN

AUSTIN MACAULEY PUBLISHERS™

LONDON • CAMBRIDGE • NEW YORK • SHARJAH

A CIP catalogue record for this title is available from the British Library.

ISBN 9781528931175 (Paperback)
ISBN 9781528966566 (ePub e-book)

www.austinmacauley.com

First Published (2019)
Austin Macauley Publishers Ltd
25 Canada Square
Canary Wharf
London
E14 5LQ

The day begins, as the sun ascends over the mountains, rays dissipating a night of darkness

Light descends across the valley, the Poisoned Glen.

Reflecting on Dunlewy Lake, peering the vacant windows or the old ruin church.

Sacred walls once echoed words of redemption, a roof that once sheltered, now open to the heavens.

Past congregations who worshipped within its walls, have now entered their promise of life eternal, for some their failed atone, certain retribution.

The morning mist slowly disperses to reveal Donegal's highest mountain; her name is Errigal, the tallest of her seven sisters.

Her majestic beauty towers over the valley below.

She kneels on the sodden grass and leans over the damp, moss-covered stone wall, then lifts her head slowly and looks over into the clearing between tall pine forests; about one hundred yards from her, a dark figure in the distance raises its head and looks in her direction.

Rain drips from the hood of her dark green oilskin coat down her flushed red cheeks; gripping the rifle tightly, her hands feel cold, almost numb as she rests the gun over the wall.

Lowering her head slowly and closing one eye, she then looks down the telescopic sight, now magnified and in focus. She can see that beast clearly as it seems to sense danger. Georgina's decision will have to be fast, a neck shot, she then decides. So much pressure all at once for an eleven-year-old girl, as she braces her small undeveloped body for such a dangerous task, the butt of the rifle pulled tenaciously against her shoulder. With her index finger on the trigger, she grits her teeth tightly. The sound of rain echoes louder as it splatters on the hood of her oilskin, breaking her concentration as she desperately adjusts her aim. Anxiety quickly sets in; her hands tremble, and her face turns pale as she tries to keep the gun steady.

That's it, she thinks and hopes that her moment is right; she then fires. The gun jolts her shoulder and the loud bang deafens her for a moment, making her lose focus through the sight; her anxiety is raised to its peak as she ponders the outcome of her shot.

"Well done, Georgie," her father Pat shouts in excitement as he looks through his binoculars and as he jumps to his feet. "Perfect kill," he says as he grins from ear to ear.

She feels pain in her shoulder from the rebound; sh lifts her head over the rifle and looks into the clearing deer lies on its side. Its legs kick for a few moments then as it breathes its last breath.

She turns her head and looks at her father as he smil her. He places his hand on her shoulder and tells her, "V done."

"She is as good as you, Pat," Jim Rodgers says as he g up on to his feet.

"Well, she had plenty of practice shooting old bean ca back at the farm. I knew she could do it," Pat replies. "We better get back, Jim, and get out of these wet clothes."

"I'll get the tractor down there," Jim says as he walk towards the main road.

Pat and Georgina climb over the wall, both wearing their denim jeans tucked into their black wellington boots, soaked to the skin from walking through the long, wet grass.

They make their way towards the deer with Pat carrying the rifle.

The morning begins with glorious June sunshine but true to its unreliable nature. Irish weather can have four seasons in one day, and it slowly turns cloudy and wet. When they get there, Pat kneels on one knee and lifts the deer's head and looks at the wound on the neck.

"She would have died instantly. You shot her through the spine. Great shot for your first time."

"I feel terrible; she is such a beautiful animal," she says, shaking her head from side to side as she looks into the deer's eyes. "Why do they have to be killed anyway; what harm are they doing?" Georgina says, not feeling very proud of her achievement.

"Well, we have to keep the numbers down, that's why we have a seasonal cull ever year."

"Why?" she asks.

"Because if there's too many when they are foraging for food, they eat all the new tree shoots," he tells her. "Be sure not to tell anyone about this. I could lose my licence if the

wrong person heard that I let a young girl like you shoot a deer."

"Don't worry, I won't tell anyone, not even Gran."

Jim drives his tractor down beside the deer, and both men grab it by the legs, then pull and slide it onto a link box at the rear of the tractor. Pat and Georgina hop on and take a lift to the main road where Pat has parked his car.

Back at Pat's farm later that evening, after a change of clothes, Jim arrives with the deer. He then reverses and parks at the shed door where both men again slide it inside.

They tie its hind legs together and use a rope and pulley attached to the rafters to winch it up with its head facing the floor. A bucket is then placed under the head and the throat cut; blood flows quickly, gravity feeds until it slowly runs dry.

After they finish, they lock up the door. Pat tells Georgina that she should get to her bed early as they plan to climb to the top of Errigal Mountain starting early next morning as a treat for Georgina's twelfth birthday.

Next morning, she is awakened by the family dog barking, completely exhausted from walking, the day before, through the forests of Glenveagh. She keeps her eyes closed. She lies but listens to hear voices as they seem to approach her home. As she listens, she recognises her cousin Bosco and his mother Mary Kelly talking outside. Suddenly, she realises why they have arrived. It is because it is her twelfth birthday.

She had lost her brother Michael and her mother Sara who had died giving birth on July 10, 1965, fourteen months after Georgina was born. She was left with her father, Pat, and his mother Peg to look after her.

The excitement of the day ahead prises her from her warm bed as she begins to open her eyes, blinking and trying to focus while the strong sunlight filters through the pores of the blue fabric curtains. This will be the day she had waited for all her young life as her father had promised to take her to the top of Errigal for the first time. Getting out of her bed, she looks for a pair of old boots that her cousin, Bosco, had loaned her for climbing the mountain. She finds them under her bed and puts them on; as they are a little big for her, she puts on a

second pair of socks. After she is fully dressed, she walks from her bedroom towards the small cold bathroom. She looks in the mirror and brushes her long, thick raven hair, then brushes her teeth. She looks in the mirror one last time before she walks towards the kitchen door. She hesitates to open the door because as she stands in front of it, she can hear her father talking to her aunt about having to take Georgina with him to live in New York in two weeks' time. She can hear him say how he could not leave her behind and at the same time felt a terrible guilt about taking her there.

After a few minutes, Georgina opens the door and smiles as she enters the room.

"Surprise, surprise," says Aunt Mary, who is sitting on a chair next to the kitchen table.

"Good morning," Georgina replies, happy to see her aunt sitting there.

"Come over and give your favourite aunt a big hug," Aunt Mary says with a smile, sitting at opposite end of the kitchen table from Georgina's grandmother.

Georgina runs with open arms towards her aunt and throws her arms around her.

"Happy birthday, Georgina," her aunt whispers in her ear. Georgina tilts her head back and smiles as she looks into her aunt's eyes. Her aunt kisses Georgina on the forehead and then tells her to look at what is on the table.

On the table is a chocolate sponge cake with 'Happy birthday Georgina' written on it in white icing, also a box of small candles in an assortment of colours. Her aunt has made the cake as she has always done for Georgina's birthdays. Granny asks, "What do you say?" prompting Georgina.

"Thank you, Aunty Mary," she says as she gazes at the cake.

"Can I put the candles on now?" Georgina asks as she takes them out of the box. The only problem is that Georgina is colour blind and can't tell the difference between reds and greens.

"Yes, go ahead, is it thirteen years old you are?" her aunt asks with a smirk as she winks at Gran.

"No, twelve," Georgina replies.

"I thought she was only ten today," says Granny, unconvincingly trying hard to keep a straight face.

"I'm twelve and you two think you are so funny," she says with a giggle.

Georgina then opens the box and sticks twelve candles into the cake one by one, in the formation of the number twelve, as her aunt and granny look on.

"When are we going to eat it?" Georgina asked.

"We will have your party after you get back from Errigal," Gran replies.

Sitting in his fireside chair is Pat. He sits combing his jet-black hair back, then standing up having a look at himself in the mirror that hangs above the fire. He is a big, strongly built but slightly overweight man who takes pride in his appearance. His mother would often tell him that he looked like actor Rock Hudson even though there was only a vague similarity between them, but he always took her comment as a compliment.

"Georgie, get your porridge in you, wee woman," Pat says, looking at her in the mirror as he fixes his hair. Georgie was his pet name for her.

"OK," Georgina replies.

"I'll get you a bowl," says Gran, as she walks towards the open fire where she still cooks even though Pat bought a new gas cooker four years earlier. She opens the kitchen dresser and takes out two bowls.

"Do you want another bowl, Pat?"

"No, you're OK," Pat replies, "I'll throw on some spuds. Will yourself and wee Bosco have some?" he asks.

"Ah, we may as well," says Mary.

Georgina, now sitting at the table, spoons some sugar on her porridge.

Gran tells her that too much sugar will make all her teeth fall out.

"She's just like her father. She has a sweet tooth," says Mary.

"She will need all the energy she can get today," Pat says as he walks out through the front door of the cottage.

"Bring in another bucket of turf on your way in, Pat," asks Gran before he closes the door behind him.

Little twelve-year-old Bosco is out playing football with Pat's sheepdog named Patch.

As the boy kicks the ball towards the dog, the dog somehow stops the ball using its mouth and then nudges it back bit by bit until it is back at the boy's feet.

"Are you having fun, Bosco?" shouts Pat, as he makes his way towards one of the outhouses.

"Yep," says Bosco. "Your dog would make a very good goal keeper."

"Do you think so?"

"Yep, he always stops the ball no matter how hard I kick it."

"It's just a pity he isn't better at rounding up my sheep."

Pat goes into the shed and picks out a few potatoes. In the shed, the dead deer hangs from the rafter by its hind legs. It soon will be butchered and sold around to a few of the neighbours. He then heads back into the cottage and begins to wash the potatoes and then puts them in a pot, ready for boiling.

In the fridge are five trout that he had caught in the lake early that morning.

He lays out all five on a chopping board and is ready to behead and clean out the internal organs. Georgina sits eating her porridge and looks over her shoulder and watches her father as he prepares the fish for dinner.

"You're going to miss this man, Gran, when he heads off to the States," Mary says.

"She says she can't wait to get rid of me," says Pat, sarcastically.

"I did not say that," says Gran.

"I am going to miss them both. Georgina was like me own daughter. There will be only myself and the dog after they go. But I can't stop them. There's nothing for them around here."

"I would love to visit Philadelphia sometime and visit the place where Dad was born," Pat says.

"What age was he when he came back here, Daddy?" Georgina asks.

"He was five years old, and because he was an American citizen, we can have dual citizenship," he replies.

"The poor man always wanted to go back himself," Gran says. "But we could never afford it when you lot were all small."

"Why did he die?" Georgina asks. "I wish I could have met him."

"He died of cancer, just like his mother," Gran says. "He was only twenty-eight."

"He left me his shotgun. He loved to go hunting," Pat says, "I suppose that's where I got the interest."

Georgina finishes her breakfast, puts on her grey duffel coat that hangs on the back of the door, then heads outside to play with Bosco.

"Do you want a game, Georgie?" asks Bosco as Georgina walks towards him.

Patch wags his tail and runs towards Georgina in an excited manner.

Georgina goes down on one knee and strokes a patch on his head a few times.

"We can take turns at penalty," says Georgina, "We will have to put the dog in the shed or he will want to play with us."

Georgina opens the shed and calls the dog in. They both play for about an hour then go back into the cottage for a drink of water.

"Look at you two with the big red faces; are you not too tired to climb today?" asks Mary

"We're OK," Bosco replies. Both drink two cups of water.

Gran is setting out the table for dinner. Pat is sitting, cutting his Condor tobacco into a large tin with a silver Condor knife he received through the post the week before by collecting tokens for over a year on the tobacco packets. Bosco, sitting opposite Pat, looks into Pat's tobacco tin. He then asks, "Why have you got that old apple in with your tobacco?"

"The moisture from the old apple keeps it fresh," he replies, as he puffs a cloud of smoke into the air.

"Can I try it?" Bosco asks.

"Try what?" replies Pat.

"Your pipe," explains Bosco.

"Your mama would kill me if I let you do that."

"You're right I would," says Mary. "There will be no smokers in my home."

"I just want to see what it's like."

"Bosco, no means no."

"That's you and I told off," Pat says with a laugh.

"You used to smoke, Mammy."

"Yes, I did until I got a bit of cop on."

"Sure, am nearly seventy and it never done me a bit a harm."

"You tell her, Gran," says Pat, keeping the banter going.

"Let's get the dinner on the table," Mary says as she finishes frying the fish

The table is moved out from the wall that is directly under a small window that has a full view of Errigal. As they all sit around the table, Gran asks them to say grace. After, the only sound to be heard is the sound of cutlery clanging around their plates, as they all quietly tuck into the meal.

"I hate fish. They are full of bones," says Georgina, breaking the silence, with a disgusted look.

Bosco bursts out laughing, almost spitting out the food from his open mouth, his mother telling him to behave himself as Georgina's frown turns to a smile.

"Give it over here, I'll take them out for you." She hands over her plate to her father who then begins to pick out the bones.

Georgina sits quietly, waiting for her father to finish removing the bones. She looks towards Errigal Mountain through the window. While she looks out, her imagination begins to wander and she imagines herself at the top of the mountain, looking down over the glen below. As she sits there, her aunt can see Georgina smile as she gazes out the window.

"A penny for your thoughts." Georgina doesn't respond. Her aunt says it a little louder, "A penny for your thoughts," as she places her right hand over Georgina's hands which are clasped together, resting on the table.

With a shocked expression and realisation that she has been caught daydreaming, she explains in an embarrassed manner, "I was just thinking, um, what it would be like at the top of the mountain."

"Ah well, you won't have long to find out," her aunt says reassuringly.

There is an air of excitement in the house that morning, at what lies ahead that day.

Pat begins to prepare for the climb and places a small pocket-sized camera in the inside pocket of his jacket.

Mary had prepared a packed lunch with a flask of tea, placed in a small rucksack that young Bosco would take with him for a picnic at the top of the mountain.

Pat reverses his car around the house and parks it at the front door of the cottage. His car is a 1969 grey mark two Cortina that had column gear change, which meant that the gear stick was attached below steering. The front seat was one continuous seat, which in turn would allow three people to sit upfront.

Pat rolls down his window and looks in the door of the white washed cottage, "Are you two ready?"

Georgina and Bosco come running out and rush around the car to the front passenger door of the car. Georgina gets in first and sits next to Pat. Mary and Gran walk out to wish them well, telling them to be careful.

They drive up to the main road, which is only a short distance from home. Along the way, Pat lets Georgina steer. Georgina leans over and grabs the steering. Pat removes his hands but is ready to take over when he feels they are in any difficulty or danger. They then arrive at the east side base of the mountain and park the car up on the grass verge.

Getting out of the car, Georgina looks up at the mountain, her heart filled with excitement. She cannot wait to get going, whereas Pat, a heavy smoker, knows he is going to have a hard time getting to the top. Bosco straps on his rucksack.

Pat leads the way towards the route up the southeast ridge of Errigal. They begin with a hike up through the boggy heather on the left side of a small stream. The going here is very wet and mushy. After about half a mile, they veer left and follow braided trails through the heather heading for the rocky trail on the slope. Once there, they begin the transition to a steep rocky trail that follows the southeast ridge of the mountain.

"Daddy, is that Croloughan Lake on the other side?" Georgina asks.

"It sure is," he replies. He then stops for a moment, "And if you look to the south of the glen, you will see the Derryveagh Mountains."

"Come on, Daddy, keep walking," Georgina says, not wanting to waste any time.

"Oh, I can't keep up with you two," Pat says panting, "We'll have a wee break half way up, then I can give you two a history lesson about the area."

They keep on climbing the small narrow trail, until they are almost halfway up and sit on a boulder perched on the slope.

"You can you see Glenveagh National Park from here," Pat says.

"Where is it, Pat?" Bosco asks.

"If you look beyond the Derryveagh Mountains, well, that's Glenveagh," Pat says, pointing over the mountains. "It used to be the domain of an English landlord called John Adair. Back in 1861, he evicted 244 tenants and cleared the land so as not to spoil the views on his estate."

"It's a good job for him I wasn't around then," Georgina says angrily.

"Why?" Bosco asks.

"Because I would shoot him, instead of shooting innocent deer," she replies smiling.

"You would be a right bit of a rebel. There would be no messing with her, Bosco," Pat says laughing.

"Pat, why do they call the glen the 'Poisoned Glen'?" Bosco asks.

"Well, I heard a multitude of reasons but the more likely explanation is that the Irish word for poison, '*neimhe*', is only one letter different from the word for heaven, '*neamh*'. It is said that the glen used to be called the 'heavenly glen' by the local people and that the English mapmaker screwed up," Pat replied. "Come on, we'd better get moving again."

They all get back on the trail and as they move further onto the apex of the southeast ridge, the landscape to the east and north also comes into view with Altan Lake far below between Errigal and the summit of Aghla More. Muckish Mountain, the site of an annual barefoot pilgrimage on St Patrick's Day, is a little further away beyond Aghla More. As they then near the summit of Errigal, Pat shows them how to surmount a shoulder where there is a large rock shelter and a cairn. From there, it is a short way up a narrowing ridge to the 2466 ft. summit of Errigal. In fact, there are two sharp peaks on a narrow ridge 25 yards apart, the trail between them being known as 'One Man's Path' as they look around the panorama on the top and take in the spectacular views in all directions. Off to the north and northwest, they can now see the Atlantic Coast and fabled Tory Island. It takes them only about one hour and thirty minutes to reach the summit of Errigal; they all collapse on their bottoms with exhaustion. Young Bosco still has the rucksack on his back, strapped over his shoulders; he slips them off and lies flat on his back. Looking up at the clear blue sky, he relaxes and feels proud that he has made it to the top.

Georgina is the first to get up and walk around, taking in the views in every direction.

"How do you feel now, Georgie?"

"I feel a little tired."

"What about you, Bosco, how are you doing?"

"Ah I'm not sure, my legs are hurting."

Pat looks at Georgina as she paces back and forth. "Is it how you imagined it would be, Georgina?" Pat asked.

"It's better, much better than I imagined," she replied.

"We could not have picked a better day. There's not a cloud in the sky," Pat says.

All three of them look down over the Glen and can see their cottage and can see a car parked near the front of the cottage. "We must have visitors," Pat tells the children. Georgina wonders who it can be. Pat lays down a blanket and asks Bosco to get the food and tea out of the rucksack. They all enjoy the sandwiches that Mary had prepared and spend about twenty minutes eating and drinking tea.

Pat takes out his camera and asks the children to smile for a photo. He then takes a few more with children in different areas of the mountain. A very enthusiastic Bosco asks Pat if he could use the camera, to which Pat happily obliges.

Pat, sitting down, reflects on his life in the glen. Thinking about the wife and child he had lost makes him feel very emotional. Georgina smiles as she sits down beside him. Pat puts his arm around her and tugs her tight into his side. This moment was very special for both father and daughter, one they would remember for the rest of their life. Pat feels his wife was looking over them; he feels he may be doing the wrong thing by taking Georgina to New York. He prays in silence for some kind of sign that he is doing the right thing.

Bosco tells them to say cheese; they both look over their shoulders with a sideways glance and smile. Bosco tells them, "1-2-3, are you ready?" snap as he takes the photo. Pat then turns his head, looks to the clear blue sky; he then closes his eye, he senses his dead wife's presence, and as if to confirm this, a butterfly lands on the back of his hand; he thinks to himself you shouldn't be up here little fellow. His eyes well up and a tear descends down his right cheek. He turns his head so that Georgina can't see it and wipes it discreetly away with the palm of his hand.

Suddenly, he stands up and says, "Will we head back?" Georgina and Bosco look at each other, one looking for the other's approval, if they should go or not. In the end, saying nothing but nodding their heads shrugging their shoulders, they agree to go home.

Going down, they find it hard to walk at a slow pace. Pat, at one time, loses his footing and rolls head over heels, luckily not hurting himself. Georgina and Bosco help him to his feet. The children can't stop laughing as Pat struggles to make his way down. It takes them only half an hour to make it back down. They then make their way back to the cottage.

At the cottage, Bosco's father Sean Kelly, his fifteen-year-old daughter Mary and two of Georgina's classmates are waiting patiently for them to arrive. Pat and the children make their way towards the door of the cottage. Pat tells Georgina to go in first. As she opens the door, a loud cheer erupts; Georgina's shocked expression turns to a relieved smile as she realises why everyone is there.

Gran makes her way forward and takes Georgina by the hand towards the table.

On the table, the candles are lit and there are all sorts of sweets. Everyone begins to sing 'happy birthday' to Georgina as she blows out the candles.

"Did you make a wish?" asks Sean Kelly.

"I did."

"What was it?" he asks.

"Not telling."

"Aha, you're not going to find out, Sean," Mary says to her husband.

Georgina's secret wish is that she and her father would be happy in New York.

All sorts of suggestions were being passed around as to what she wished for, but Georgina let everyone know that they were all wrong.

Sean, an accomplished musician, has brought his accordion. He begins playing and singing.

The party goes on till late. Gran retires to her bed at ten; Pat has had too much to drink and fell asleep on his chair. Bosco spots an opportune moment to play a prank on Pat.

He puts all the empty Guinness bottles on his lap and then takes a photo, one he could use to embarrass him with at a later stage.

Everyone enjoys the evening. Georgina thanks everyone for a great night.

Going on twelve and everyone is going home. The parents arrive to pick up Georgina's classmates. Mary tidies up and persuades Pat to get to his bed. Sean and family are the last to go. Georgina locks up, turns off the lights and goes into her bedroom.

She sits on her bed and takes out a photo of her mother that she keeps in her bedside locker. She thanks her mother for a great day and reassures her that they will be together one day soon. She then lays back and before she can remove her boots, she quickly falls fast asleep.

A week has passed since the climb. Pat has sold off most of the sheep during the prior six months and is loading the remainder of his sheep onto a trailer with high cribs hooked onto a tow bar on the car. He then will take to Milford mart to sell, which is about twenty-five miles away from the glen. A neighbour called Jim Rodgers, who has a mobile butchering business, is helping Pat and will go with him to the mart. Jim intends to rent Pat's land when he emigrates.

Georgina is helping bake scones with Gran. Gran is an excellent cook and has taught Georgina everything she knew. Georgina relaxes in Pat's fireside chair while the scones bake. As she sits there, she reminisces about all the good times she has had here, and as she looks at her Gran hobbling around the kitchen, she wonders how she will manage when they've emigrated. Gran asks Georgina to switch on the TV for the six o'clock news.

They sit and watch the RTE news until six thirty, then turn it to the BBC news.

As they watch, a photo of a convicted murderer is shown. He has murdered a young girl in London and was given a life sentence.

Gran looks at his photo and says, "Look at those eyes; he has no soul, that man." Georgina looks at the man's photofit on the TV, puzzled by what Gran had just said.

"What do you mean when you say he has no soul?"

"The eyes are a window to a person's soul. Some have no soul, just like the man on the TV who had no mercy for the young girl he murdered."

"Can you tell this by looking into anybody's eyes?" Georgina asks.

"Sometimes you can tell a lot about a person by looking into their eyes," Gran replies.

"Let me look into your eyes, Gran."

"OK, I'll take off my glasses first," says Gran.

"What do you see?"

Georgina looks for a moment and smiles, then replies, "Only your blue eyes, Gran."

Gran puts her glasses back on, laughing as she does so.

"You're too young yet to understand, young girl."

Gran gets up then walks over to the oven and takes out the scones from the oven, sets them on a wire rack on the table to cool. Georgina makes tea for both of them.

While eating one of the scones, Georgina asks, "Have my mum's and brother's souls gone to heaven?"

"Your mum was a kind and beautiful person. She would have gone straight to heaven."

Georgina stops chewing her food and with a blank stare, tears stream down her face.

Gran hasn't noticed and asks her if the scone tastes good. With no reply from Georgina, Gran looks at her and sees the tears running down her face.

"Are you OK?"

With a lump in her throat, she tries to reply in a weary voice, "I'm fine."

Gran is concerned by this, because normally she is a strong-willed little girl never showing weak emotions. She pats her on the back.

Suddenly, Georgina sits up and runs to her bedroom.

Gran shouts, "What's wrong, wee woman," a few times. Georgina doesn't reply.

Gran, who has arthritis, makes her way slowly to Georgina's bedroom.

She looks into the room and Georgina is lying face down on her bed.

Gran makes her way over and sits on the bed beside her and says.

"Sit up so I can give you a hug."

Georgina slowly gets up and wraps her arms around Gran, resting her head on Gran's shoulder crying uncontrollably

Gran pats her on the back and whispers, "It's OK, don't be crying, wee woman."

"I wish my mum was here, not in heaven. God shouldn't have taken her from me."

"Everyone in school has mummies except me; it's not fair," she says, her bottom lip quivering.

"I understand, but it was God's will. You will be together again someday."

Georgina takes out the photo of her mum from her locker and sits and looks at it with Gran.

"She was a beautiful woman, your mother. I miss her too. You know she would not like to see you crying like this."

"I'm sorry, Gran," Georgina says.

"Don't be sorry; it's only natural. It's good for you to get it out of your system, having a good old cry," Gran says.

Georgina stands up and smiles through the tears. Gran takes out a tissue and wipes them off.

"Help me up, wee woman."

Georgina giggles as she tries to pull Gran up from the bed.

The sound of a vehicle approaching the house can be heard in the distance.

"It's Andy," Georgina looks out her bedroom window and says, gushing with excitement.

Andy drove a mobile grocery shop; he would arrive once a week.

Georgina always looked forward to him coming around as Gran would buy her sweets and crisps.

Gran fetches her notebook from the press. She has a list of groceries that she needs.

"Take this out and give it to Andy, I'll be out in a minute."

Georgina rushes out with the book, running towards the rear steps of the van.

"How's my wee darling," says Andy, as Georgina steps in the back of the van.

"I'm good, Gran will be out in a minute," she hands the notebook to him.

"Watch this," Andy throws a blue milk of magnesia bottle that is used for indigestion onto the table. It bounces but doesn't break. A bewildered Georgina gasps as the bottle hits the table. She lifts the bottle up and examines it.

"It's plastic," she says with a bewildered look upon her face.

"Did I scare you?" Andy says, laughing at her reaction.

"You did, I was not expecting that, I thought it would break."

Gran makes her way into the van.

"Hello, Andy, how are you doing?"

"I'm very well, Miss Boyle, thanks for asking."

"Look at this Gran, a plastic bottle," she says, handing the bottle over to her gran.

Gran then has a look at the bottle and realises that it is plastic and taps it on the table.

"Glass bottles will soon be a thing of the past, Miss Boyle."

"This is a great idea, Andy," Gran replies.

"This will be the last time I'll see Georgina, Miss Boyle; is it Monday they're off, is it?"

"That's right, they're off to the United States. The lucky things, I wish I could live my life over again and I would go too."

Andy gives Georgina a free packet of sweets, £2, as a birthday present and wishes her safe journey to America.

Later that night, Pat arrives back at his house with Jim Rogers. They had been drinking in a pub in Milford town that evening. Jim who was driving is lucky he didn't crash as he makes his way home. Jim tells Pat as they walk into the house that he is going to butcher the deer in the morning. He then bids them goodnight and leaves. Gran wasn't impressed with Pat and tells him to sit down before he fell down. Pat sits down in his chair and sings Danny Boy at the top of his voice. Georgina puts her fingers in her ears to let him know how terrible he sounds.

When he starts again, she goes over places her hand over his mouth and tells him to be quiet. Pat apologies to both of them, gets up and he then staggers to his bed.

The next morning, Jim arrives. Gran invites him in for a cup of tea.

"Is the big man not out of his bed yet, Mrs Boyle?" Jim says, sipping his tea.

"Not yet, Georgina has taken him down a cup of tea; he shouldn't be too long now," she replies as she sits at the table.

"Good morning, Jim; Daddy is getting up now," Georgina says as she walks into the room.

"He's a bad boy, your daddy, Georgina; when you grow up, don't drink," Jim says.

"I won't, not after looking at Daddy this morning," she replies.

"Are you going to help me butcher the deer this morning, Georgie?" he asks.

"No, definitely not, but I might watch you do it all the same," she replies.

"Ah, look who it is; well, how's your head this morning, big man?" Jim asks Pat when he walks up from his bedroom.

"Can you not tell by looking at me?" Pat replies. "No breakfast for me this morning, mam, straight to work on this deer, Jim."

"Yes, sir, Sergeant Pat has given the orders. Come on, Georgie, straight to work, and thanks, Mrs Boyle, for the tea."

Jim opens the back door of his black Morris minor van. In the back, he has a fold-up table, a hacksaw and a set of butcher knives. Georgina and Pat help him carry them into the shed where the deer is hung.

Georgina watches as Jim first skins the deer and then cleans out all the internal organs. She tells them that she has seen enough and goes back into the house.

Later that day, Pat takes in a few pounds of the meat to cook for dinner. He and Jim share profits on the sale of the rest of the meat as Jim would sell it to his regular customers.

It's Sunday, the day before they emigrate. All three of them are at Mass.

During Mass, Father Gallagher asks the congregation to pray for Pat and Georgina that they would have a safe trip to the USA. He also talks about Pat, telling how much he will be missed, as he was a great tradesman and had done a lot of work for everyone in their community. After he has finished talking, everyone stands up and applauds.

For Pat, it seems to go on forever; he feels humbled and slightly embarrassed by the attention.

When outside, almost everyone comes over and wishes them well; some slip Georgina loose change. They then make their way to the graveyard to the family grave to pay their respects. Georgina and her father know it will be a long time before they will be back here again.

Later at the cottage, they both pack their bags as they will get up early next morning.

Gran gives them some Gartan clay to place in their bags, which is blessed and protects anyone who carries it when they travel.

That night, all of them find it hard to sleep, tossing and turning through the night.

Six a.m., the alarm rings in Pat's room. He gets up and puts on the kettle.

Gran then gets up, followed by Georgina who is groggy, still not fully awake.

As they eat their porridge, Sean Kelly arrives at the house. He is going to drive them to Dublin Airport, about a four-hour journey. He has a cup of tea while he waits for them to finish breakfast. Pat puts the suitcases in the back of Sean's car.

"Time we got going," says Pat.

Gran asks Georgina for a farewell hug. They stand and hold each other tight for over 3 minutes. Pat hugs and kisses Gran, tells her to look after herself; he then makes his way towards the door, blesses himself, then is followed by Georgina.

Gran looks emotional as they walk out the door.

In the car, they wave goodbye to Gran as she stands in the doorway like a dark shadow against the light shining in the kitchen behind her…

As the car travels away, Georgina keeps looking back and waving at Gran, even though she, at this stage, cannot see her.

"God help Mam, am I doing the right thing at all Sean?"

"Don't worry, she's a lot tougher than you think," says Sean.

"It's just the age she is now, if anything ever happens to her, I would never forgive myself."

"Don't you be worrying yourself like that, Pat. We're never too far away."

Gran sits alone in the cottage; it's only now she realises how lonely she will be.

She sits at the fireside and she says her morning prayer, hoping the loneliness will pass.

Even though they've only left ten minutes ago, she looks around the empty room.

She realises that because of her age, they may never see each other again.

As they travel across the border into Northern Ireland, they are stopped by British soldiers. Sean is asked to open the boot of his car by one of the soldiers. Another soldier taps on the front passenger window. Pat rolls down the window. The soldier asks him his name and where he is travelling to. Pat explains that he and his daughter are travelling to the USA that day.

Sean isn't too happy about being stopped and expresses his Republican views to Pat.

As they reach Monaghan town in the Republic, they stop and have some fish and chips.

It takes another two hours before they reach Dublin Airport.

In the airport, Pat and Georgina say their goodbyes to Sean.

Neither Pat nor Georgina have been on a plane before and don't know what to expect.

Georgina takes the window seat. Pat is a big fellow and looks a bit cramped sitting beside her. The time comes for take-off; the plane accelerates up the runway, and it's not long before they are high in the sky.

Pat leans over Georgina and take in the views, both of them are thrilled by this new experience. Five hours later, the plane lands at JFK international airport.

It's mid-June and the temperature is 89 degrees Fahrenheit with high humidity.

As they leave the plane, they are hit with the searing heat outside.

"It's so hot, Daddy."

"I know, I wasn't expecting this."

"I'm going to take off my jumper," says Georgina.

"I think I'll do the same."

After they get through customs, they collect their bags. Waiting at arrivals is Pat's sister Susan. She is a nurse in Mount Sinai hospital in Queens for over 12 years.

It had been over five years since she was in Ireland and she doesn't recognise Georgina when they meet.

As they walk out of the airport into the strong sunlight, it burns like a furnace on their pale skin. Pat has never experienced these temperatures before and is already thinking this may not be for him. Susan is thrilled that she has her younger brother and niece in New York.

"How can you stick this heat, Susan?"

"Don't worry, Pat, after two or three weeks you won't notice it."

"How are you doing, Georgina?" asks Susan

"I can feel my skin burning."

"I have air conditioning in my car; it's in this car park."

Susan tells them to put their bags in the trunk and get into the car; she then drives up the Van Wyck Expressway away from the airport. Pat is overwhelmed by the size of the motorway and how many cars are on it.

"It's strange sitting here and the steering being on what should be the passenger side," Pat remarks to Susan.

"Do you remember teaching me to drive back in the old sod, Pat?"

"I do indeed; I also remember how sore you were on the clutch; I think I had to replace it not long after you headed off to America."

"I'm so sorry. Georgina, do you hear your father? He still hasn't forgiven me after all these years."

"It's OK, I brought the bill with me, and it's in my back pocket," Pat says jokingly.

"How do you put up with him, Georgina?" Susan asks, glimpsing Georgina through the rear-view mirror with a smile.

Georgina smiles, looks up and can see her aunt in the mirror; she replies, "I just don't listen to him."

"You're my kinda girl, Georgina," her aunt says, laughing.

As they travel in the car and takes in the views of what seems like an alien world to them, they both have a lot of admiration for Susan who has made this country her home.

They travel up Roosevelt Avenue under the number seven line.

Georgina, saying nothing, is wondering what the red steel structure elevated along the street is above her.

They then are stopped at traffic lights at Woodside when the sound of a subway train is heard, taking off.

"What is that noise?" asks Georgina.

"That's the subway train above us. It's heading for Manhattan," Susan replies.

"How do you get up there?" asks Georgina.

"There are lots of stations with steps up to them, and when it goes underground, there are steps down into the stations also."

"Can I go on it sometime?" asks Georgina.

"Yea sure, I will bring you and your pop into Manhattan tomorrow; I'll give you guys the grand tour of the city."

They turn right at Seventy-Third Street, Jackson Heights. Susan owns a house there, and she has been living there for over five years.

The house was divided into three apartments. Old Miss Green rents the top floor of the house with Susan in the middle and the basement to be taken by Pat.

She parks her car in front of the house.

"Well, here we are; I'll get you two a cup of good old Irish tea when we go in."

"It's a fine-looking place you have here, Susan. It's a credit to you."

"Well, thanks. It could do with some of your handy work, Pat."

They make their way up the steps into Susan's apartment. Susan tells them to put down their bags inside and she would show them the basement later.

As they sit and talk about old times, Susan gets them some cool drinks; she then puts on the kettle for tea.

Beads of sweat roll down Pat's face. Susan looks at him, shaking her head, and tells him to get into a tank top. He tells her that he has one at the bottom of his bag, so Susan shows them down into the basement so they can unpack.

They go outside and up the side of the house to a side door that goes down into the basement apartment. Susan gives Pat two sets of keys and tells him to open up.

Pat turns the key, opens the door and walks in, followed by Georgina. What they see is a large room with a small kitchen on one side and two beds at the other side.

Susan then walks in and takes them to a doorway near the kitchen that leads into a small shower room. There is also a large boiler that heats the house.

"Well, do you like it, Pat?"

"It could not be better," he replies.

"It's a very big room," says Georgina.

"I hope that you can divide it up, Pat, whenever you get the time."

"I'm looking forward to getting started."

Susan tells them to unpack and that they have a wardrobe each. She then takes out a small foldable divider that she places between the beds to give Georgina and Pat some privacy while they change for bed at night. They both pick their beds and unpack.

As they are unpacking, the phone rings; Susan has had a connection put into the basement from her apartment.

"Hello."

"Hi, Mary, they are here safe and sound. I'll put you on to Georgina."

Mary rings to make sure they have arrived safely and is happy to hear Georgina's voice on the other end of the line. Pat also has a quick word and talks about his concern for his mother being alone at home.

"Pat, you know as well as I do that your mother is very much set in her ways," Mary says. "To ask her to move out of her family home at this time in her life, well, you know, Pat, she would never agree to it."

"I know you are probably right, Mary, but try your best to persuade her. It's been playing on my mind since I left," Pat says, upset by the thought of his mother alone in the cottage.

"Pat, just give it a little more time and she will realise that she will be lonely living all alone, and that there are certain things that she can't do without help, but don't worry. I'll call around and try and convince her to move in with us."

"Thanks, Mary. I won't keep you any longer; I'm only putting up your phone bill."

"No, you're grand, just you and Georgina look after yourselves."

After he has finished the phone call, they make their way back up to Susan's apartment where she has prepared bacon and cabbage with Idaho potatoes for them. This is Georgina's favourite dinner.

"I love your potatoes, Susan, they're very tasty," Pat says.

31

"They're from Idaho; they're very popular here," she replies

"This is my favourite dinner, Susan, I love bacon," Georgina says.

"I know, and I also have banana ice cream with jelly for dessert," Susan replies.

"You two don't realise how great it is for me to have my own flesh and blood here with me. It just feels so good to have you here."

"You know, Susan, it's great to be here and see how the other half lives," Pat says. "You seem to have lost your Donegal accent; there is only a wee twang of it left."

"It happens, if you worked with Americans for as long as I have, you would end up with just a wee twang left yourself, Pat. Can you imagine your father going back to Donegal with a Yankee accent?"

Georgina's giggles turn to laughter, shaking her head to say no.

She shows them around her apartment that originally was a family home but has been divided into three separate apartments by the last owner.

Going on five o'clock, she decides to take them for a walk, to show the way to the subway and nearest shops. The subway station is at the end of their street. She takes them up the steps and shows them where to buy tokens; they also get a few subway maps.

She then takes them to The Poteen Irish bar for a drink. The bar also has a shop selling Irish imports and Irish newspapers. Working in the shop is a dwarf called Mick; everyone calls him little Mick. He always jokes with customers that he was a leprechaun in Ireland and couldn't get any work back home.

They sit up at the bar. Pat has a pint of Guinness which he really enjoys as he says that it tastes as good as you would get back at home. Susan and Georgina have a bottle of coke each. Susan explains to Pat to leave his money on the bar, and he will get every third drink free from the bar. Everyone in the bar is Irish and most had just finished their day's work.

Pat has noticed three men coming up from the basement. They were doing renovations in the bar. They sit up at the bar beside Pat. Five minutes later, Pat gets talking to them.

He explains that he had just arrived and if they knew where he could get some work.

One of them called Tom told him he could start on Monday if he was prepared to help dig out the basement by hand, as there wasn't enough height and that it was being converted into a party room by the owner. With no hesitation, Pat accepted his offer and shook Tom's hand. Pat bought the three men a drink and left a tip for the barman before they left.

As they walk back, Susan congratulates Pat on getting some work as he had been only in the country a few hours. Pat couldn't believe his luck; even though it was digging, he thought to himself it would lead to better things.

When they arrive back at the house, they all sit down on a bench beside Susan's front door. They listen to sounds of cop car sirens and traffic.

"It will take you two a while to get used to the sound of the traffic in your beds at night," says Susan.

"Does this go on all night?" asks Georgina.

"It certainly does; remember, you're in the city that doesn't sleep, but you get used to it; after a week, you won't notice it."

"It's still very warm, even when it's dark; is it like this all night?" asks Pat.

"Yes, all night, but it's not as hot in the basement. I'm going inside to get you two a nice cool drink."

Sitting on the bench, Pat and Georgina talk about their new experience; how very different their lives would be compared to the one they left behind as Susan hands them both a cool drink and asks their opinion on it, not telling them what it is.

"It's nice," Pat says, taking another sip and trying to analyse it. "Is there lime in it?"

"I give up, what is it?" asks Georgina.

"OK I'll tell you, it's tea, what they call iced tea with lime."

"It's the coolest tea I've ever had," Pat says, laughing as he takes another sip.

"Iced tea is popular in America as it quenches your thirst better than soft drinks."

Next door, a little girl on roller skates stops and looks over the fence.

"Hi, Susan," she says.

"Well, hi Maria, I'd like you to meet my niece; her name is Georgina, from Ireland."

"Hi, Georgina," Maria says, waving her right hand.

"Hello, Maria," Georgina says smiling.

"Can I take Georgina over and show her my bedroom, my dad has just finished decorating it for me?"

"Would you like to go over, Georgina?" asked Susan

Standing up, Georgina hands her glass to Susan.

"How long can I stay there?" Georgina asks.

"Come back in about an hour, say nine thirty. Maria, will you look after her?"

Georgina follows Maria towards the back of her house. Susan tells Pat how her next-door neighbours had moved from Brazil in South America three years ago.

Susan suggests that they go inside; she then gets Pat a late-night snack.

"Jesus, Susan, they know how to make fridges over here," Pat says as he opens the door of a large American-style fridge. "I could fit in there myself."

"They like to build things big here," she replies as she finishes frying some leftover potatoes for Pat.

"I'm happy to see Georgina will have that wee girl to play with; it might help her settle here," Pat says as he tucks into his snack.

"Maria is only six months older than her; hopefully, they will be in the same class up in St Sebastian's school in Woodside. It's only a fifteen-minute walk from here," Susan says as she sits, sipping her coffee. "Maria's mom will take her there and collect after school, so you won't have any worries. Their home is set up just like my own, divided into three."

"She will look after her until one of us gets home. She is a real good person and is not too expensive."

Georgina arrives home, accompanied by Maria.

"Hi there, you two," Susan says as they enter the kitchen. "Did you have a good time, Georgina?"

"Yes, I like Maria's bedroom, it's very pretty," she replies.

"Good night, everyone, I'd better get home," Maria says.

"I'll take you over, Maria and thanks for looking after Georgina," Susan says.

Both Pat and Georgina wish Maria goodnight and decide to go to the basement; both of them, at this stage, are very tired and go to their apartment to retire for the night.

They both feel hot and sweaty, trying to sleep that night. At one time, they hear the sound of gunshots in the distance, which scares them a little. Georgina is so exhausted that she doesn't stir that night; even her father's loud snoring doesn't wake her.

In the morning, Pat has a shower. This is the first time he has ever used one. In an overexcited manner, he then wakes Georgina and tells her that she should try out the shower also.

As Georgina stretches her arms, she looks around the room and thinks to herself, *I'm in America, I'm in America.* She smiles as she looks at her father sitting on the small sofa whistling an unknown tune and tying up his shoelaces.

After Georgina has showered and dressed, they go up to Susan's apartment. She has invited them both up for breakfast where she had prepared bacon and eggs with toast. Susan wants to get into the city early so she could fit as much in as she could that day.

They board the subway at Jackson Heights' station, Georgina has never seen any other race of people before; in the train, there are people from every corner of the world.

As they travel towards Manhattan, the train goes underground, under the Hudson River; both of them find it a little scary at first, but exciting.

The first place she takes them to is the Empire State Building. Pat has his pocket camera with him and takes lots of photos of the outstanding views of New York. Later that day, they take a boat to the Statue of Liberty.

As they leave the boat and walk on Liberty Island, Susan explains that the statue is made completely of copper and that it was a gift from the French government in the year 1884.

They climb the spiral staircase inside the green corroded copper structure, all 354 steps to the crown. Inside the crown, there are 25 windows that look out across the river. The sun is beginning to set and there is a beautiful red sky that reflects across the river. Unfortunately, they move on as there are more people waiting their turn at the viewing points.

They also go to Ellis Island; this is where Pat and Susan's grandfather and grandmother would have arrived when they travelled to America all those years ago.

Back in the city, she takes them to Times Square as their final destination that day.

There are a few unsavoury people around, and she thinks it best that they leave.

Back in Jackson Heights, Susan takes them for pizza near the subway station. Neither Pat nor Georgina have had pizza before.

"Do you like it, Georgina?" asks Susan.

"I love it," she says, finding it difficult to hold in her hand, and take another bite.

"Hold it like this, just fold it in a U-shape, like I am doing now," explains Susan.

Georgina and her dad soon get the hang of it.

Pat sits quietly watching Georgina and how happy she seems. He feels so lucky to have Susan to come over to.

"Thanks, for a great day; I really enjoyed seeing the sights. What did you think of the city, Georgie?" asks Pat.

"I really liked the Empire State Building; I remember watching it on TV back at home when King Kong climbed to the top of it."

"I didn't think you would remember that film," Pat says.

"I watched it with Gran about a year ago. She said it was her favourite film."

"That's a really old movie. Gran will be at Mary's house tomorrow; we will be talking to her on the phone. You can tell her about the Empire State Building. She will be so pleased to hear that you were there," Susan says.

"Will we head back? You two must be tired now," Susan says.

"Well, I am beginning to know what jet lag means, I'm feeling really tired now," Pat replies.

They walk back to each of their apartments. Susan kisses Georgina good night and tells them to be ready for Sunday Mass leaving at nine thirty; she will be driving to St Sebastian's Church up in Woodside next morning.

During the night, Pat's snoring wakes Georgina.

"Shush, you're snoring. Can you be quiet?" Georgina says in a whispering voice.

Pat sleeps, oblivious to Georgina's frustration. She asks him a few times, but in the end, she gets up and shakes his shoulder.

He sits up quickly. "What the hell is wrong?" Pat says, sitting up, a shocked expression on his face.

"You are snoring; I can't get any sleep. I tried to tell you a few times, but you just didn't hear me."

"I'm sorry, you remind me of your mother; I used to keep her awake too. If I start again, tell me and I will take my mattress into the boiler room and I'll sleep there."

"OK, I will give you one more chance," Georgina says, getting back into bed.

Pat then finds it hard to get back to sleep as he becomes self-conscious and hopes he wouldn't snore again.

True to form, Pat was snoring again. Georgina sits up, her bottom lip squeezing tightly against her top lip, in a temper, hops out of bed and marches to the shower room.

She rolls two pieces of toilet tissue and stuffs them in her ears.

She then struts back to her bed, grabs her covers and pulls them over her head.

Next morning, Pat remembers how he had wakened Georgina during the night. He looks over and he smiles when he sees the tissue in her ears.

Georgina wakes up in a bad mood when she sees her dad.

"You snored again," she says.

"Sorry, I will sleep in the boiler room from tonight until I divide up the basement, is that OK?" he says.

"I'm sorry for shouting at you, I'm just so tired," she says.

They both get ready for Mass and go up to meet Susan for breakfast. They take the car up Roosevelt Avenue under the subway line towards Woodside.

St Sebastian's chapel is beginning to fill up but as it nears the time for Mass to start, Pat remarks that it is almost half empty. Susan explains that it used to be a cinema; that is why the floor is sloped towards the altar.

Pat can recognise all the Irish faces in the congregation. He then thinks he spotted an old school mate sitting on his right-hand side; this was someone that he had not seen in years. He whispers to Susan did she know him. Susan says that she didn't know him.

When Mass finishes, Pat insists that they wait outside so he can talk to him. Luckily, the man walks out the same exit.

"Hello, Jim," Pat says, standing on the steps outside the main door.

"Hi there, I know your face, I just can't put a name to it," the man says.

"Pat Boyle, from the Poisoned Glen."

"Ah, Jesus, I should have known you; long time no see," the man says, grabbing Pat's hand and shaking it.

"I don't recall seeing you around here before, or are you here on a holiday?" Jim asks.

Pat explains that he and Georgina have moved to New York to live with his sister. He also wants to talk about old times, so Jim suggests going to Dolan's bar in Woodside, which was only 100 yards away. Susan says that she would go back and cook lunch.

Jim shows Pat all the Irish haunts as they walk down the street towards Dolan's Bar.

They walk into the bar; Pat is surprised how many people are in there so early in the morning. The owner of the bar, Pat Dolan, gets them a drink.

Pat Dolan was from Donegal Town and was well known by the Irish community in New York for helping new arrivals from Ireland find work.

Mr Dolan tells Pat that if he ever needs any work, he has plenty of contacts in the construction industry. He also tells him all how the Woodside to Sunnyside area have been taken over by the Irish community.

The three men talk about good and bad times back in Donegal. Georgina listens intently but is steadily growing tired.

"Can we go now, Daddy?" Georgina says, with a dull expressive look upon her face.

"I think we'd better, Susan's dinner will have gone cold at this stage."

"We can take the train, Daddy; I know where to get off," she says, her face breaking into a smile.

"Well, Jim, it was great to meet you again," Pat says, getting up from his stool, "I'll take your phone number. Sure, we'll try meeting up again, sometime soon."

"Well, I live up in Sunnyside; if you ever need anything, just give me a call," Jim says.

They then part company and Pat lets Georgina show him the way back on the subway.

Back at Susan's house, Pat knocks at the door.

"You two made it back OK," Susan says.

"All thanks to Georgina. She knew the way back; she's a quick learner, my girl," Pat says.

"I easily used this little subway map," Georgina says, showing Susan her map.

"Good girl, I've kept both your dinners warm in the oven as I knew your dad would find it hard to leave the bar."

Susan had prepared roast chicken with a barbeque sauce with broccoli and backed potatoes, followed by cheesecake for dessert.

During the meal, Susan tells them that Gran will be calling from Ireland at four o'clock. After they finish their meal, they move to the sitting room and watch TV. Pat remarks to Georgina that they seem to have adverts every fifteen minutes.

They had never seen colour TV before. They switch through a few different channels, then at four o'clock the phone rings and Susan answers the phone.

She talks to Gran, asking how she was doing; after a few minutes, she calls Georgina to the phone.

"Hello, Gran."

"Is that you, Georgina?"

"Yes, guess where I was yesterday?"

"I don't know, I suppose you'd better tell me."

"The Empire State Building; I was at the top floor. Remember you said that King Kong was your favourite film and you said that you would like to go there sometime?"

"I do, I'm just glad that you have been there. How do you like New York?"

Georgina is overcome with excitement and tries to tell her Gran every detail of her new life in America. Gran listens but can't get a word in edgeways.

Pat also talks to Gran; she admits that she feels lonely since they left, and she will move in with Mary. Pat feels relieved to hear her say that, as he is the one who advised her to do so.

Gran wishes them well; she is so happy to hear that Pat already has work lined up and is happy to hear Georgina's voice again. They agree to keep in touch by phone at least once a week.

Pat tells Georgina that Gran is moving in with Mary Kelly's family.

"What about my dog?" Georgina asks. "Will he be moving too?"

"He will, and he'll probably find the move more difficult than Gran," Pat replies.

"Will we head up for the Donegal papers? They will be in the Poteen shop now," Susan says.

They decide to walk to the Poteen Bar as it is only four blocks away.

Near the subway, as they are passing, there are two men; one of them whispers, "Coke Cane-Coke-Cane-Coke cane."

Susan tells Pat. "Don't look, don't answer him, keep walking."

Pat was taken aback by Susan's reaction and waited until the men were a safe distance away until they were out of earshot.

"What the hell was that all about?" he asks.

"I'll tell you later, not in front of Georgina," she replies, walking a little faster.

"Why did that man keep saying coke cane to you, Susan?" Georgina asks.

Susan is reluctant to answer Georgina, but she then thinks she'd better tell her.

She then stops walking; her eyes roll then look up as if in deep thought.

"Those two guys are drug dealers; you just ignore them as I do. Jackson Heights is known as the drug capital of the world, so we have to be careful. That's all I've got to say on the matter, now let's go," she takes Georgina by the hand and tugs her along.

Pat is still standing, then asks Susan to stop. Susan just keeps walking.

"Susan, stop," Pat asks, raising his voice and pacing quickly up behind Susan.

"Listen to me, please stop," he asks in an angry tone.

Susan then stops. "What more do you want to know?" she says.

"What do you mean by saying this place is the drug capital of the world?" Pat says.

"This could have waited until later, but if you need to know right now, most of the drugs distributed around the world come here first then move on. Do we really have to talk about this in front of Georgina?"

"It's OK, Aunty Susan, I don't mind," Georgina says.

"Sorry, Susan, I was just taken aback by what you said," Pat says in a remorseful way.

"How about we go and get the papers and I will buy Georgina a packet of Oatfield sweets that came all the way from Letterkenny," Susan says smiling at Georgina.

They soon make their way to the Poteen and go into the Irish imports shop.

Pat spots the Donegal newspapers.

"It's hard to believe. I can pick up my local paper a short walk from my apartment here, and if I was back in Donegal, I would have to drive five miles for them," Pat says as he reads the headlines in one of the papers.

"How are you, Susan?" Little Mick says with a great big smile.

"I'm doing great; I must introduce you to my niece, Georgina."

"Well, hi there, Georgina, it's so great to meet you," Mick says.

"Hello, it's nice to meet you too. Why are you so small?" Georgina says curiously.

"Georgina, you shouldn't ask a question like that. I'm so sorry, Mick, and I'm her father, Pat," Pat says, embarrassed by what Georgina said.

"Georgina, you ask me anything you want; don't you listen to your pop, and if you would like to know, I was born this way," Mick says.

Mick and Pat talk more. Mick explains how he too had moved to America from Mayo with his parents and sister when he was just five years old and how his father opened the Poteen Bar over ten years ago. He told Pat that he was lucky to get work with Seamus as they would be doing a lot of work in the Poteen Bar over the next two months.

Back at the house, Pat and Georgina go to the basement. Pat has a read through the papers and they both retire to bed at ten o'clock as Pat has an early start.

Next morning, Pat takes Georgina to the child minder next door. Mrs Rodriguez asks Pat if Georgina likes Irish stew as she said she would cook it for Georgina to make her feel more at home. Pat just laughed and asked where she learned how to cook Irish stew. She said his sister Susan taught her how to cook, and it was originally his own mother's recipe. Pat couldn't believe it and said his mother would be delighted if she knew this.

Pat strolls up the street towards the Poteen Bar. He gets there early and sits on the door step watching people walk by, then at about eight o'clock, Seamus and his brother Tom arrive in a black Ford Transit van and park outside the main door.

"How are the two Letterkenny men doing?" Pat says, getting to his feet.

"Not so bad," Seamus says, getting out of the van. "Do you smoke, Pat?" Seamus says holding an open packet of Marlboro towards Pat.

"I do, but I never tried Marlboro before; back at home, I used to smoke the pipe."

Tom goes across the street and gets coffee for them. Seamus shows Pat into the basement. They would have to dig about two feet out by hand to give a little more headroom. Seamus is waiting for another Letterkenny man to turn up, called Joe Nee, and explains to Tom that he is a heavy drinker and that he is engaged to an Italian American called Maria and would be getting married in four weeks' time.

He says that her family wasn't happy about her getting married to Joe as her father had links with the mob.

The three of them begin digging and carrying the soil in buckets up through a side door to a skip parked on the sidewalk. Joe turns up at ten with a massive hangover; his hair is a mess, and he hasn't shaved for a few days, and his scrawny body due to his heavy smoking makes him look even worse.

"You're late again, Joe," Seamus says, in a bad mood.

"I'm dying, too much Guinness last night."

"Grab a shovel; we'll soon sweat it out of ye," Tom says.

"Maria will soon put a stop to these big benders that you go on," Tom says, picking on Joe. "Ye have four weeks of freedom left."

"Don't worry; no woman will tell me what to do or what not to do," Joe says, looking the worse for wear, sweat running down his forehead, then after a few minutes, strips to his waste.

"I tell ye one thing, Pat, all them days digging turf done you no harm; take it easy; you're making us look bad," Seamus says.

Seamus is impressed with Pat and instinctively knows that he was going to work very well with his men.

They dig out most of the soil that day and within a week are deep enough and are ready to lay the concrete floor.

They then began to divide out the basement as a party room with a bar and men's and ladies' toilets. Seamus assigns Pat to work with Joe, but as usual, Joe has a habit of not turning up, leaving Pat to do a lot of the work on his own.

Pat is an excellent carpenter and Seamus is now able to leave Pat in charge while he is out doing other work.

Pat was never as happy; he is doing the work he loved and getting very well paid for it. Then after the third week, he gets a pay raise. He is now earning more in one day than he could get for a week back in Ireland.

With his new pay raise, he decides to take Susan and Georgina for a meal in the steak house in Woodside on Sunday after Mass.

"Thanks, Pat, this is my favourite place to come for a meal. You will enjoy the steak in here. Waiter!" Susan says, raising her hand to catch a young man's attention.

"I couldn't afford steak back home. I was only good at catching fish. We probably would have starved otherwise."

"Hi there, what will you have on the menu?" the young waiter says with a smile.

"Georgina, will you have steak like your pop?" Susan asks.

"Yes, please, can I have ice cream after?"

"Of course, you can, sure, Susan is paying for it all," Pat says with a wink and a smile.

"If I have to pay for it, there's a good chance we end up washing all the dishes."

"Can we have three 6 oz steaks, well done?" Susan says handing back the menu to the waiter.

During the meal, Pat explained that he was invited to Joe Nee's stag do starting in Dolan's Bar at four o'clock.

Most of the men at the stag do would be from Letterkenny, and he was afraid that it could get out of control when they had too much to drink.

Susan told him to go, as he could make new friends, but he should leave if there was any sign of trouble.

"Can I have a banana split?" Georgina asks.

"Why not, what about you, Susan, will you have the same?" Pat says.

"No, I'll have another glass of red wine. Why don't you try a glass, Pat? It helps you digest the steak," Susan says.

"Sorry, but I might leave you two here, it's nearly four. I was in two minds whether to go to the stag night, but I'd better go, as he has invited me to his wedding next Saturday."

"Go on, Pat; enjoy yourself, just don't you overdo it. Dolan's is 200 yards from here," Susan says.

"I'll be on my best behaviour, what about you? Will you be OK on your own?" Pat says.

"I've been here for 12 years; I think we will manage."

Pat gets up and kisses Georgina's forehead. He hands Susan a $100 note to pay the bill. Susan jokes could she keep the change; Pat tells her to give it to Georgina for her piggy bank.

Walking towards the bar, he felt anxious as he did not know what to expect.

Then as he got closer, he could hear the singing through the open door.

Standing inside the open door, Pat looks around for Joe, at the other side of the dark oak bar are a bunch of men; they all seem to be having a good time.

"Pat, over here," a voice called out among them. "A hand appears, waving, above their heads, and again a voice cried out, "Pat, over here." Pat then recognises that it was Tom calling him over. A song came on from a jukebox by Van Morison, called Brown Eyed Girl, as Tom looked around; Joe was standing putting money into the duke box. He hadn't noticed Pat.

"How are you, Joe?" Pat says, putting his hand on Joe's shoulder.

"Jesus, Pat, you made it. Joe says putting his arm around Pat, resting his hand on Pat's shoulder; his voice slurred and pulling Pat in the direction of the group of men that Tom is with.

"Come over here with me too; I'll buy you a fucking drink, ye big fecker ye," Joe says pulling Pat among the men.

"Look who has just arrived, Seamus, the big Donegal man himself," Joe says pushing his way into the middle of the group.

"Well, Pat, you're a late starter. This is Pat Boyle from the Poisoned Glen everyone, if any of you lot need a good carpenter, Pat's your man. Isn't that right, Pat?" Seamus says sitting on a high stool at the Bar.

"Mr Dolan, a drink for Pat here," Joe says.

"When did I become Mr Dolan, what happened to my first name?" says Pat Dolan – owner of the Bar.

"It will be Pat from now on," Joe replies, then says, "There's too many Paddys in here. Look up at the other end of the bar, there's Galway Pat, and back at that table behind us is Dublin Pat. What will we call this new man then? I know, how about big Pat?" Joe says.

"I don't care what you call me as it's not early in the morning," Pat says, everyone laughed at his comment.

A kitty was formed with everyone putting $50 into a jar. There were twenty-four men in the group, most of them from Letterkenny. Tom was driving the van and wasn't drinking alcohol. They had planned to go to the Poteen bar next but Joe had other ideas.

"Boys, will we go to Honey's strip club?" Joe says, staggering slightly, holding on to the edge of the bar.

A cheer erupts from the men, "Drink up, boys, and we'll go," shouts one of the men.

"Joe, I couldn't go to that place," Pat says with a concerned tone.

"Ah, come on, Pat, it will do you the world of good," Joe says.

"No, I'm not going," Pat replied.

"Come on, boys, let's get this man into the van," Joe says lifting Pat's arm around his own neck, then a few more gather around him, lifting him off the floor and rush towards the door. Pat protested on the way out, but knew he had no choice as they bundled him into the van.

The men were all crammed into the van with Tom and Seamus sitting in the front. They head up Queens Boulevard, they then pull up outside Honey's nightclub.

As the back doors of the van open, a large cloud of cigarette smoke escapes along with the men as they scramble their way out one by one.

"Don't you think you're staying here, Pat?" Joe says grabbing Pat by the arm and pulling him up from the floor of the van.

"God you're a devil; I'll go in if it pleases you," Pat says.

The group make their way into the club; the music is very loud. Pat reluctantly is the last to go in. By then, some of the men are standing around the bottom of the stage that runs up the centre of the tiger stripe decorated and darkly lit room, where a semi naked girl is dancing provocatively.

Pat walks towards the Bar and gets a drink. Tom is standing with his hands in his pocket. He looks around and sees Pat standing at the Bar on his own, and he walks over to see if he's OK.

"What do you think of this place, Pat?" Tom asks with a cheeky glint in his eye.

"Not much, if you want to know the truth," Pat says, sipping a drink from a bottle. I can't wait to get out of here. I don't think marriage will settle Joe; he's as mad as a March hare.

"I think you're right," Tom says. "But he's going to have to watch himself; his girlfriend's family have strong links with the mob. They'll not put up with his kind of behaviour. The problem is, I think he's marrying her for her money. She already owns a house in Howard beach."

"I think you could be right. Just look at him. Does he look like a man that's getting married next week to the girl of his dreams?" Pat says, shaking his head in disbelief as he watches Joe waving dollar bills to the girl on stage. "He has invited me to the wedding, you know, I don't know if I will go or not."

"Why not, sure myself and Seamus will be there. We'll look after you," Tom says.

Susan and Georgina went to the Poteen shop that evening as the Donegal newspapers are due to be delivered there after seven.

Little Mick was on duty as usual, entertaining customers with good old Irish humour and jokes.

"Well, hi there, Susan, and I see you have brought that cute little Irish girl, Georgina, with you. Boy, is she gonna have a hard time fighting off all the guys when she's older. But don't worry about it. I have the same problem with the girls. Your aunty Susan always looking for a date with me, I'm afraid I always turn her down." Mick says, giving a cheeky wink and laugh to Georgina.

"You're terrible; don't ever believe a single word he says, Georgina. I thought you would be at the stag party tonight," Susan says.

"Sorry, Susan, I ain't crazy. A little guy like me wouldn't stand a chance drinking along with Joe; he doesn't know when to stop."

"Yea, my brother, Pat has been telling me all about him. I hope he settles down when he's married. His girlfriend must see his good side or she wouldn't be marrying him," Susan says.

Susan and Georgina walk home. On the way back, they meet a male and female cop on foot patrol. Georgina notices that the female cop is carrying a gun, and as they pass her by, she turns to look at the gun.

"I'm going to be an army woman when I grow up," Georgina says, looking up at her aunt and waiting for her reaction.

"An army woman, hmm, did you decide that just now?" Susan asks curiously.

"Well, kind of, when I was back in Ireland, I thought of being an army girl because you get to use guns, but I think I would like to be an army woman if I live here."

"Do you like guns? They're very dangerous you know, your dad would be worried if you did a job like that," Susan says.

"Daddy knows I want to join the army. He even let me shoot his rifle when we would go hunting," Georgina says with confidence.

"Well, it will be a few years before you can join the army. You may even change your mind and want to be a nurse like me."

They make their way into the house; Georgina will sleep on the sofa, as they don't know what time Pat will make it home.

At Honey's nightclub, Pat decides to go home, Tom tries to get his brother Seamus to leave too. Seamus is very drunk at this stage and needs help out to the van.

On the way to Pat's apartment, Seamus falls asleep.

Tom gives Pat the keys to the Poteen bar, as he knows that Seamus will leave him late to work the next morning.

That morning, Pat is woken by the alarm clock. He sits up; his mouth is dry, his head in a thumping pain. He groans as he lifts his feet and places them on the floor. He then struggles to stand up, staggering towards the sink and fills a glass of cold water.

He is so dehydrated he drinks three glasses of water.

"I'll never drink again, never," he says to himself, as he dresses for work.

He then makes his way to the deli across from the Poteen bar and buys a coffee.

He sits near the window and sips on his coffee, watches the Chinese owner use an abacus instead of a cash register. He is amused by this, as he hadn't seen one in use since he was at national school. He wonders about this man and how he had left China just like himself and made New York his home.

Feeling a little better, he decides to go across to the Poteen and get some work done.

He begins working on building the new bar in the basement. At eleven, Mick and his father turn up to open the bar and shop.

"Hi ya, Pat, how's your head this morning?" John Gibson asks.

"Not good, but I'll survive, I hope."

"Come upstairs, Pat, I'll give you the hair of the dog," Little Mick says.

"God I never drink at this time of the morning."

"Come on, one drink, it will cure you," Little Mick says.

Pat sits at the bar and John gets Pat a pint of Guinness. As he sits talking to John, in walk Seamus and Tom.

"I see you're having a liquid breakfast, Pat," Tom says.

"I'll have one of them as well, John," Seamus says.

"I got a little bit of work done on the bar; I might let you finish it off as you have a clear head."

Seamus sits with his head face down on the bar and tells the men that he can't remember a thing about the stag do, and that they probably won't see Joe for a day or two.

They struggle to work through the day and finish early.

"There's someone knocking at the door, Aunty Sue, will I answer it?" Georgina asks.

"Yea, answer it, I'll be there in a minute."

"It's Daddy, Aunty Sue, we got the Donegal papers for you, Daddy."

"Good girl yourself, thanks Susan for looking after the wee girl last night."

"It was a pleasure; you're home early, are you OK?"

"We were all in bad form today. Seamus let us finish early."

"Where did you all end up?" Susan asks.

"You wouldn't want to know, Sue," Pat says, shaking his head, cringing with embarrassment.

Pat talks about the night before while having dinner but leaves out the fact that they ended up in Honey's. He promises

Georgina that he will make a start, dividing up the basement and give Georgina her own bedroom.

Back at work the next day, Joe doesn't turn up for work that full week. The only thing they hear is that he had been seen drinking in a bar in the Bronx.

They try his apartment every day after work, but he is never in.

Tom helps Pat divide the basement after work. Pat lets Georgina help nail on the plasterboard.

The morning of the wedding, Pat puts on his newly pressed black suit. He sits on the bench in front of the house, and he waits for Seamus and Tom to give him a lift to the wedding, As he sits there watching people walking by, he thinks about his friendship with Seamus and Tom and how they seem to look after him, for which, he is grateful.

Tom goes to an old aunt who lives in Woodside. He keeps his car locked up in her garage as he never really uses it that much.

They then pick up Pat and make their way to the church on Howard beach. They arrive early to see if Joe has turned up.

As they arrive at the church, a few men walk over and ask who they are; Tom explains that they were invited by Joe. One of them asks where Joe is as he had not arrived yet.

Tom, worried by Joe not being there yet, gets out of the car to see if any of the Letterkenny boys are inside. He then meets a few of them – Johnny McGinty who is the best man. He told him that Joe had been drinking with a few Letterkenny boys late the night before up in Sunnyside.

Tom rushes back to the car and tells Seamus and Pat that he was going to Joe's apartment to see if he was still there. He realises that Joe would be in big trouble if he is late.

At the apartment building in Sunnyside, they rush up the stairs to Joe's apartment and bang their fists on the door. He does not answer and they are not even sure if he is there or not.

The old Greek guy who lives next door asks what the hell are they doing.

Tom explains that Joe is supposed to be getting married and they are not sure if he is in or not. The Greek guy rings the attendant to see if he has a key to let them in.

After five minutes, he arrives and opens the door and they rush in.

"Here he is," Tom says, after finding Joe sleeping on the sofa. "He's drunk as a skunk, the stupid bastard. Damn him anyway, how the hell is he supposed to get married in another hour?"

"Settle down, Tom; try slapping him around the face," Pat says.

"I'll punch him in the face, that's what I should do, wake up, Joe, damn you. Joe, will you fucking wake up?"

"Why are you filling the bath, Seamus?" Tom asks.

"I'm going to give him a cold bath that will wake the bastard up. Come on, strip the clothes off him," Seamus says.

"Where is his fucking suit, you go look for it, Pat, we'll put the bastard in the bath."

Pat looks everywhere but no sign of the suit. Seamus and Tom strip Joe and dump him, straight into the bath of cold water.

"Fuck, fuck, fuck, what are you doing, are ya trying to drown me?" Joe says, grabbing the side of the bath, pulling himself up into a sitting position, shocked by the cold water.

"You're supposed to be getting married, what the fuck were you thinking, going out drinking last night?" Tom says in an angry tone.

"A couple of the lads called 'round and asked me out with them."

"Did you ever learn the word NO? That's what you should have said," Seamus says.

"Where is your suit? I can't find it anywhere," Pat asks.

"It's in the dry cleaners, I intended to get it yesterday, but I forgot all about it," Joe says, standing up shivering with cold. "It's probably closed at this time of the morning."

"Tom, your suit will fit him, we've got to hurry."

"What the hell am I supposed to wear then?"

"Whatever you can find."

Tom takes off his suit, shirt and tie. Joe puts them on, and they don't quite fit, but he has little choice. Seamus gives him a strong cup of coffee. Tom finds some clothes in Joe's wardrobe and puts them on.

They rush down the stairs and into the car; after five minutes, Joe feels sick and they stop. He puts his head out the window and throws up.

They are now half an hour late. As they drive up, a younger brother of the bride walks towards their car and taps on the front passenger window where Joe is sitting.

"You'd better have a good excuse for being this late, no one does this to my sister," Giovanni snarls. He then can smell the booze from Joe's breath, "You're drunk."

"No, I just had one to settle the nerves; it's not every day you get married," Joe replies, realising he is now in big trouble.

"Get in there fast, you're making my family look bad. There are a lot of important people here today."

The four of them make their way to the back door of the church. Joe thanks Tom for getting him there. Tom tells him to hurry up to the altar. He is very unsteady on his feet and feels that all eyes are on him as he makes his way to the front of the church.

On the left are the Italians and on the right, the Irish. It wasn't hard to tell which was which as the Italians all wore expensive clothing and jewellery and Maria's father had splashed out a lot of cash on flowers to decorate the church for his daughter's special day.

Everyone can see that Joe is still drunk. It is not going down very well with Maria's family, but they just grin and bear it.

The bride and her father make their way up the aisle as the organist plays *Here Comes the Bride*.

Joe's cousin, Johnny, the best man is the only close family member who attends the wedding.

While the wedding is in progress, there is a lot of whispering about Joe and the condition he is in.

After the ceremony, photos are taken, and the bride's father takes her to one side. He tells her that he is disappointed in the way Joe turned up for the wedding and how this will reflect on the family.

"I thought you said he was going to give up the booze," Maria's father says angrily.

"I'm sorry, Papa, he promised me he would stop drinking," she replies.

"I'll pay for treatment if you agree to send him to a clinic," he says.

"Thanks, I'll talk to him tonight at the hotel. I know he will do it for me," she says.

"Good then, after you two get back from your honeymoon, I will arrange for him to attend the one up near our holiday home in the Catskills," he says.

The reception didn't go that well either, as Joe began drinking again and had to be carried out by Tom and Pat. To make matters worse, one of the Letterkenny boys got into a fight with Giovanni, who pulled out a gun and told him that he would have him killed.

Tom and Pat take Joe to the Waldorf Astoria Hotel in the city, where he was to spend the first night of his honeymoon but now without his new wife.

"What an idiot, I thought he would know better than to drink again," Pat says sitting in the front passenger side of Tom's car.

"Don't talk to me, I should have known better," Tom says full of anger. "You couldn't trust him as far as you could throw him. I just thought he would have more sense in front of her family."

"It's not your fault, I can see her divorcing him very soon. He has no sense at all," Pat says.

"We'd better pull in and get a coffee into him or they won't let him into the Waldorf," Tom says.

They stop at a deli in Manhattan and make Joe drink two coffees before they take him into the hotel. On the way back, Tom tells Pat that Maria wants Joe to get treatment and her father would pay for it.

At nine o'clock next morning, Joe is awoken by a knock on the door from room service. As he comes to his senses, he is baffled as to where he is. He looks on the bedside locker and there is a card with the Waldorf Astoria written on it. He begins to remember certain things about the day before. He doesn't recognise the clothes that he wore in bed that night.

Again, there is a knock at the door with a male voice saying, "Room service." Joe makes his way to the door and opens it.

"Breakfast for Mr and Mrs Nee," the man says.

"Thanks, come on in," Joe says. "You wouldn't happen to know if my new wife is in the hotel or not?"

"Why don't you ring reception? They could help you with your enquiry."

Joe begins to worry why she isn't with him. He has no appetite and struggles to eat some of the breakfast. At 10 o'clock, there is another knock at the door.

He opens the door and Giovanni and his older brother Leo, also known as Leo the butcher, are standing there.

"Hi, Joe, can we come in?" Giovanni says.

"Sure, come right in, where is Maria? I know I fucked up yesterday, I'm sorry."

The men walk into the room saying nothing, close the door and sit down.

Leo was Giovanni's younger brother; he was known as Leo the butcher. He sits and stares with a grumpy look on his face.

"You fucked up is an understatement, I came here to inform you that Maria doesn't want to see you unless you can stop drinking for good," Giovanni says.

"Can you tell her I'm so sorry? I'd do anything to turn back the clock. I know I do have a problem," Joe says, fearful of what lay in store for him, as he had heard rumours about Leo having killed two guys in Brooklyn in his past.

"Maria booked you into a clinic up in the Catskills this morning. She will only agree to see you again if you go there and get dried out," Giovanni says.

"No problem, I'll do anything; I'll give it a try."

"Well, let's go; we'll take you straight to it. We also have a holiday home nearby that you can use. If you want my sister back, you have got to do this."

"I would need to go by my apartment to pick up some clothes and some cash," Joe says, with the intentions of contacting by phone, some of his friends, just in case anything happens to him.

They leave the hotel in Leo's car, Joe sitting in the back seat. The atmosphere in the car was cold; Joe felt uncomfortable about what lay ahead for him.

"Thanks for taking me up here," Joe says but with no response.

"I could get a loan of my friend's car and save you two guys the bother of having to drive all the way up there." Again, he gets no reply from either of the brothers.

They then stop at his apartment complex in Sunnyside. The brothers sit in the car as Joe rushes up the stairs to his apartment and changes into a new set of clothes.

He then phones Tom who lives just a few blocks away. He wants to let him know where he is going. Tom warns him not to go, but Joe feels he will lose Maria if he doesn't go.

They drive nonstop Upstate until they reach the Catskills. It takes about two hours to get there. At the clinic, Joe is booked in and they then go for a meal in an Irish diner.

Joe still doesn't feel comfortable sitting, eating with the two men. They had barely ever spoken to him in the past two years he had known them. Leo hadn't spoken a word to him that day. He felt they were up to something, but he couldn't figure out what they might do. During the meal, Joe tells the two men that when he collected his clothes in his apartment, he rang to say that he was travelling with them to the clinic up in the Catskills. He thought, by telling them this, it would stop them from possibly killing him, if that was their intention.

He noticed Leo looking sideways at Giovanni still chewing on his food, with a grumpy frown on his face. Giovanni places his knife and fork on each side of his plate, then glances towards Leo, then towards Joe.

"What friends did you tell?" Leo asks with a face on him like a bulldog.

"I just called a few of the guys that I drink with," Joe replied, now knowing that they intended on possibly killing him.

"Did you not think you should have kept quiet about it? This isn't something you boast about to your friends," Giovanni says in anger.

"Well, I thought that if anyone was looking for me, it would be better if they knew where I was," Joe says.

"Do they know that we're with you?" Leo asks, his face frowned in anger.

"Yeah," Joe says with confidence, knowing he had undermined their plans.

"Let's get the fuck out of here," Leo says wiping his lips and throwing the napkin on the table.

"We'll leave you back at the clinic," Giovanni says, standing up.

They then drive back to the clinic. As Joe leaves the car, Giovanni asks Joe if he would like breakfast in the morning, as they were going to stay in the holiday home nearby and do some fishing. Joe agrees to meet up with them.

In bed that night, Joe dwells on his behaviour and how he must have looked in front of Maria's family. He remembers how Maria had begged him a few days before the wedding to ease off on the drink. He closes his eyes and vows to himself that he will change but his thoughts turn to the wedding again and how hard it will be for him to be accepted by Maria's family.

Next morning, Joe gets up, takes a packet of Marlboro cigarettes and goes outside for a smoke as he paces back and forth outside the gateway entrance to the clinic. Giovanni and his brother turn up in Leo's black Mercedes car.

"Hop in," Giovanni says in a pleasant manner, as he sits on the front passenger side.

"Sure," Joe says, and then opens the rear passenger door, getting into the back seat.

"How's treatment going?" Giovanni asks, looking over his shoulder with a glancing smile.

"Ah, we had an introduction last night. We were asked to admit that we were all alcoholics as we all sat in a circle in a small room; I hated doing it," Joe replied.

"Maria will be pleased to hear that. I'll call her and let her know," Giovanni says.

They drive for about a mile and they reach the holiday home. They go inside and have some breakfast that Giovanni had prepared earlier.

Joe begins to trust his new brothers-in-law; he felt that they couldn't just kill him.

He looks out through the French doors at the back of the house and can see the lake.

"That's a fine view of the lake you have here; is it any good for fishing?" Joe asks.

"Yeah, it's great for fishing. We've got a small boat out there, and how about we cast a few before you go back?" Giovanni says.

"I'd love to, I haven't fished in years, and the last time I fished was back in Ireland, in the local river called the Swilly," Joe says.

"There's great big fresh water trout. You can take one back to rehab," Giovanni says, laughing.

Leo just sits eating at the table looking at his plate, with a miserable expression, as if he wished he was anywhere but sitting in Joe's presence.

Giovanni gets up first and takes the plates towards the sink for washing up, leaving Joe sitting at the table with Leo.

Leo sits, chewing the side of his gum, tapping his figures repeatedly on the table, his brows frowning down over his dark blue eyes, avoiding any eye contact with Joe.

"How's your demolition business doing these days, Leo?" Joe says with a nervous tremble in his voice.

Leo sits saying nothing for a moment, turning his eyes and looking away from Joe, then replies, "Great, fucking great." He then gets up, shoving his chair back angrily, then walks towards the French doors. He unlocks the doors and goes outside, walking towards the boat on the lake.

"He's pissed off today, Joe," Giovanni says as he washes the dishes.

"I'm sorry for dragging you two up here," Joe replies.

"It ain't because of you," Giovanni says laughing. "He got a few business problems. You may have hit a raw nerve asking him about our demolition company."

"Sorry, I shouldn't have mentioned it," Joe replies, shaking his head from side to side.

"Don't worry, he'll be OK once he's out on the lake for a few hours; it'll calm him down," Giovanni says, as he fixes his greased, receding brown hair, looking at his reflection on the glass door that leads to the hall. "Come on, let's go out on the lake and you can teach me how to fish," Giovanni says, slapping his hand down on Joe's shoulder.

Joe gets up from his chair with a smile. He thought to himself that Giovanni was being genuine and was trying to help him quit the booze.

They walk through the white French doors to a paved path, through overgrown grass that leads to the boardwalk on to the lake. The lake was surrounded by trees that reflected on the still water around the perimeter of the lake.

It was a beautiful morning, and Joe was beginning already to feel the benefits of an alcohol-free diet. It was his first morning in over a year that he hadn't had a hangover.

They then make their way to the 14-foot boat; it has a small out-board motor.

Leo is sitting in his long mauve Crombie with matching hat at the back of the boat.

He sits smoking a cigar and ignores the men by looking away as they step down onto the boat.

Giovanni sits at the front, Joe in the middle, then Leo stands up and pulls the pull start on the outboard motor a few times until it starts.

He steers it out to the middle of the lake and then turns off the motor.

Joe starts to feel uncomfortable as the smoke from Leo's cigar slowly passes in the still air.

He tries to convince himself that Giovanni is on his side and that he would never allow Leo to harm his sister's new husband.

"Grab yourself a rod there, Joe," Giovanni says as he takes a swig of whiskey from a silver flask he had taken from his jacket inside pocket. "I would offer you a drink, only my sister would kill me if she ever found out," he says, laughing, putting the flask back into his pocket.

Joe just smiles as he casts his line into the water. He sits, knowing that Leo is sitting directly behind him, but as he looks in the calm water, he can see Leo's reflection.

He seems to just sit there, as if he was enjoying the tranquillity of the lake.

Joe breathes a sigh of relief and begins to reminisce about his childhood back in Letterkenny when he would go fishing, with Tom, Seamus and their father Tomas.

Tomas had a rowing boat and they would spend hours every Sunday fishing in the Swilly River.

Joe and Giovanni cast their lines, but Leo just sits staring at them, saying nothing.

Joe feels a tug on the end of his line.

"I got one," Joe shouts.

"Good for you, reel him in," Giovanni says.

Leo hops up from his seat, then quickly places a wire wrapped around both of his hands over Joe's head, then quickly wraps it around his neck and begins to choke him.

The rod falls into the lake and Joe falls backwards, his head against Leo's knees.

He tries to get his fingers under the wire, but it is so tight, he can't.

He tries to shout 'help' but a croaking sound is all he can do. He looks up into Leo's evil eyes and claws his face in a desperate attempt to stop him.

"You fucking Irish bastard," Leo shouts. "Grab his fucking hands."

"I'll shoot the bastard," Giovanni says.

"No, grab his hands; I don't want his blood all over my clothes," Leo shouts.

Giovanni grabs Joe by his wrists and pulls them away from Leo's face.

Joe begins kicking Giovanni. This angers Giovanni, and he lunges his foot into Joe's chest a number of times.

Joe's face turns blue and his body goes limp. Leo still keeps a tight grip on steel wire that is now cutting into Joe's neck, blood running on to the collar of his shirt.

Dormire con i pesci stasera.

"You'll sleep with the fishes tonight, you drunken Irish fucker," Leo says in Italian, and then drops Joe's head on to the floor of the boat. He then stands up and begins kicking Joe's lifeless body.

"Stop, he's dead. Let's dump his body before someone sees us."

"I've had to come the whole way up here, to whack this dumb mother fucker, and we could have wasted him back in New York," Leo says in anger.

"Pop wanted him whacked up here. We have to make it look like he committed suicide; if we dump him here, he'll never be found anyway," Giovanni says.

Under a blanket on the boat, they had hidden two concrete blocks, with blue nylon rope tied around them, one they then tied to his feet and the other around his neck

They then lift his body and drop it over the side of the boat then throw over the concrete blocks.

The weight of the blocks drags his body straight to the bottom of the lake.

Leo then drops the steel wire into the water.

Twenty-four-year-old Joe, who had come to America for a better life, now lies dead at the bottom of a lake.

Life had never been fair for Joe; at five years of age, his father died from a chest infection, brought on from years of breathing coal dust as he unloaded the coal boats with a shovel on the Swilly River.

His mother, who had suffered from depression, ended up in the mental hospital.

Joe was taken in by relatives and Tom's mother also had looked after him in later years.

The Gallagher brothers asked him over after they had established their business in New York in 1970. They trained him in carpentry when he got there.

They would call him the *Aer Lingus* carpenter as a joke, because he had no qualifications before he had left, and seemed to have served his apprenticeship on the flight on the way over.

On the way back, Giovanni discusses with Leo what they would tell their sister Maria. Their plan was that they left him at the clinic and they travelled straight back to New York that day. They would tell her that he felt suicidal because of what he had put her through at her wedding. They also knew that no one had seen Joe get into the car with them that day.

A week has gone by; Tom decides to try and find out how Joe was doing in the clinic.

He calls the pizza house on Howard Beach where Maria is a manager and asks her if she had been in contact with Joe. She tells him that she had been warned by her father not to make any contact with him until he completes his treatment. She then gives him the number of the clinic and tells him to let her know how he is doing.

Tom calls the clinic; he asks to speak to Joe Nee. The lady on the phone tells him that Joe only stayed one night, and he had left, leaving a bag of clothing. There was also a small sum of money in a drawer that belonged to him.

Tom knows something is wrong; he decides to ask Pat and Seamus to help him search for him. He calls around to Pat's apartment and tells him about his concern for Joe. Pat agrees to travel with him to the Catskills and help search for him. Seamus decides that he would look after the business. Tom then makes a call to Maria and tells her the news. When he tells her, she begins to break down and cry. She then tells of her fears, that her family never liked Joe, especially Leo, and that he could be capable of anything. Tom asks her to file a missing persons report and that he would search for him with the help of Pat.

Later that Sunday evening, Pat tells Georgina that he could be away for a few days and that she would have to stay in her aunt's apartment until he returned.

He also is concerned for Joe as he had worked with him for over four weeks and had grown to like him and also his great sense of humour.

They leave New York in Tom's car; its Pat's first time travelling Upstate, and he remarks that there are times when he looks around the countryside, and he feels that he is still in Ireland. Late that night, they arrive and book into a motel for the night.

Next morning, they go to the clinic. The lady in the clinic tells them the cops came the day before and took statements from her and the rest of the staff that were on duty the day that Joe went missing. She had been informed by Maria, who phoned that morning that Tom was to take back the clothing and money he had left behind.

Tom asks her if Joe had been seen with anyone suspicious the day he vanished.

She tells him that Joe seemed to have vanished early that morning. He never turned up for breakfast. But this was not unusual as lots of them quit, never finishing their treatment.

Tom confides in Pat that he feels only a small glimmer of hope that Joe may still be alive. They drive to a diner for breakfast. Tom makes a call to Maria and asks directions to their family holiday home, so that he could check that he was there.

They get there in less than five minutes. Pat reckons that he could have walked there easily. But Tom says, even if he could, he would not have left his clothes and money behind. They park outside the cedar clad house. Maria had told Tom that he would find a key for the front door hidden under a small concrete slab on the right-hand side of the door. They let themselves in and then look in each room. They could see no sign of Joe having been there. Pat looks into the fridge; the only thing in it is a packet of butter and two bottles of beer.

They go through the back French doors that lead to a wooden deck with a small boardwalk leading out to the lake. As they walk towards the lake, they see the small boat tied onto a mooring. Tom steps on to the boat and looks for any sign that it was used lately.

"If they killed Joe, they did it here," Tom says as he scans his eyes across the lake.

"It's hard to know; he could be back in New York, sitting on a high stool, drinking, having a good laugh at us all," Pat says.

"He's now missing a week; if he was alive, he would have called me," Tom says in a stern voice.

"Only for Joe, I wouldn't be alive. I can't swim. When I was twelve years old, we were out fishing and I fell into the river. I was trying to pull in a great big salmon."

"All I remember is being swept down under. I began inhaling water. My whole short life passed before me, and the next thing I know, someone was pulling my hair and dragging me up. My head broke through the surface, and I gasped a lung full of air. I look and there's Joe pulling me towards the bank. He was only eight years old and the scrawniest little bastard you ever seen, but at that moment, he became my hero. I never thanked him for it." Tom struggles to control his emotions and gasps looking to the heavens as if looking for some kind of inspiration or help from above.

They talk for over an hour, Tom telling stories of all the good times he spent with Joe. He tells Pat that from the first moment Joe drank alcohol, he was hooked and spent almost every night drinking.

They decide to drive back to New York that night. Tom asks Pat to drive even though he hasn't got a licence. Pat finds it difficult at first but after a few miles, he gets used to driving on the right-hand side of the road.

When they reach Yonkers, they try a few of the bars and ask the bar staff to watch out for him. They do the same around the bars in the Bronx as Joe was well known there. Once they reach Queens, Tom drops Pat off at his apartment. He tells him to take the next day off.

In the morning, Pat knocks on Susan's door. Georgina looks out through the sitting room window, and to her delight, her father is standing, waiting for the door to be opened.

"Come in if you're good looking," Georgina says, laughing as she opens the door.

"My God, your sense of humour is getting worse than my own," Pat says, walking in and lifting Georgina up in his arms. Georgina puts her arms around Pat and hugs him tightly with a great big smile.

"What have you been up to since I've been gone?" Pat asks, lowering Georgina to the floor.

"Susan and I went to the Bronx Zoo yesterday. It was brilliant, and the monkeys were so funny to watch," Georgina tells Pat, excitedly.

"You're so lucky, I haven't been to a zoo yet, and would you go again with me some day?"

"Hi, Pat," Susan shouts from the bedroom, the door opened slightly, "I'll be with you in a moment."

"Did you find your friend?" Georgina asks, "And why is he hiding anyway?"

"No, and I don't think he's hiding anywhere," Pat replies.

"Why is he missing then?"

"I'd rather not tell you, Georgina. I am going to Susan for a moment. I just want to talk with her on her own, is that OK?" Pat asks.

"That's fine. I'm going to get some breakfast anyway before I go to my child minder," Georgina says.

Pat knocks on Susan's bedroom door. "Can I come in?" he asks Susan.

"What's up?" Susan asks. "I heard you talking to Georgina about him.

Pat closes the door behind him and sits on the end of Susan's bed as Susan puts on her makeup sitting in front of her dresser looking into her mirror.

Georgina carries a bowl of cornflakes in milk with her and stands outside the door, listening with curiosity.

"We looked everywhere," Pat says. "He's been missing for over a week now. Tom is in a bad way about him; he feels responsible for him."

"He shouldn't, it's not his fault," Susan says. "Joe was a grown man. He should have known what he was getting himself in for; that girl's family is linked with the Mafia," Susan says in an angry tone.

"I guess you're right, but I think Tom will still feel responsible," Pat says with his head bowed down as he stares at the floor in deep thought.

"I might go to work later. Tom says that I could take the day off, but it might take my mind off what happened," Pat says.

"Pat, this is a great country to live in, as you know, but if you're looking for trouble, it's only around the corner," Susan says, looking back at Pat in her mirror.

"Have some breakfast here, Pat," Susan says. "You can make me a nice cup of coffee when you're in the kitchen."

"Thanks, I would need to go out and do some shopping later on," Pat says. "I will take Georgina to Mrs Rodriguez after breakfast."

"Don't worry about the shopping," Susan says. "I'll be back early, and I'll do it for you. I also promised Georgina I would take her to a clothing store and buy her a pair of denims and a few tank tops."

"Thanks, Susan. You're one in a million. I'll get you that coffee."

As Pat makes his way to the door, Georgina tiptoes quickly to the table with her food and sits down, just before the door opens. Pat walks out and gives Georgina a smile, unaware that she was listening to their conversation.

He makes Susan a cup of coffee then takes Georgina next door.

He then walks to the Poteen bar. It was a beautiful morning, and as he walks along the path, he looks up at the clear blue sky, his thoughts turn to where Joe could be.

Suddenly, he bumps into Little Mick.

"Sorry, God, I'm so sorry," a shocked Pat says, realising he had almost knocked down Mick.

"Steady on there, big fellow," Mick says, smiling. "You should look down. Sometimes there are little guys like me down here."

"My mind was somewhere else, I'm sorry," Pat says.

"Don't be sorry, just be careful," Mick says grinning. "I'm only kidding, big man."

"Is Tom working at the bar this morning?" Pat asks.

"Yeah," Mick replied, "The two Gallagher brothers are working in the basement. The mood isn't good. I think they're worried about Joe, and if you ask me, they have every right to be. I heard of that Leo Corbally – also known as Leo the butcher – and his family. It's well known that the son of a bitch killed two guys in Brooklyn two years ago; it was on the news, but he had a good alibi. You could say he got away with murder."

"I met his brother Giovanni at Joe's wedding; all I can say about him is I wouldn't like to mess with him."

When Pat arrives at the Poteen bar, Seamus is at the side of the building throwing rubble into a skip, sitting by the sidewalk.

He tells Pat that Tom has started building the bar in the basement and that Liam Diver, another Donegal man, has started wiring in all the lighting.

Pat makes his way down to the basement. Tom is surprised to see him as he had given him the day off.

Both men work on building the bar. They were working with solid oak planks and cutting them down to size. Tom was now able to have Pat take over as he was an excellent carpenter; this is something he couldn't do before as Joe was prone to making mistakes. Tom never worked with plans but relied on paintings that were done by an Irish artist, based in Manhattan, who portrayed leprechauns drinking in bars; Tom would recreate sections of the bars that were depicted in the paintings.

By lunchtime, they head across the street to the deli where the old Chinese guy worked.

As usual, he uses an old abacus to count up the cost of the food. Everyone has a lot of respect for him for sticking to the old ways and culture of his country.

They are joined by the electrician Liam Diver. Liam has been living in New York for fifteen years and has six children. He left Ireland when he was sixteen years old and served his apprenticeship there. He was a man of few words. He had been late that morning and never said why; Tom was curious and decided to ask him.

"You were late this morning, Liam," Tom asks.

"Yeah, I sure was," he replies.

"Did you sleep in or were you and your missus trying for another kid?" Tom says, poking fun at the man with few words.

"Ah, I was off getting married and a few things this morning," Liam replied sarcastically, as he had got married in a registry office early that morning.

"Married and a few things, you say?" Tom says, surprised by his reply. "I was wondering why you were wearing a pair of nice shiny shoes to work."

"Why was I not invited?" Seamus says. "Had you anybody invited, ye tight whore ye?"

"No, just me and the good lady herself; three would be a crowd and as you know, I don't like crowds," he replies.

"That poor woman, how does she put up with you?" Tom says. "Where are you taking her on honeymoon?"

"Well, I might take her to Central Park for a walk and then for a slap-up meal at McDonald's after," he replies, full of sarcasm.

"Well, it's about time you done the right thing, look how long you kept her waiting," Seamus says patting him on the back.

"O she's a lucky girl; I'm a very good catch," Liam replies.

"Yeah, you're a good catch as bait for a shark," Seamus says, laughing.

All four men sit in the deli laughing and keep poking fun at Liam, who has a very dark sense of humour.

When they were back at work later on, Tom had been searching for a Stanley knife in a large lock up toolbox. In it, he finds Joe's belt on a nail bag; as he lifts it up, a small bottle of Jack Daniels whiskey falls out and bounces on the floor. Tom thought that Joe seemed to be tipsy on a few occasions, but he never caught him drinking on the job. Seamus says he thought he was making lots of mistakes lately but put it down to all the late nights.

Joe's name wasn't mentioned during the rest of the week, but he remained in each of their thoughts and the hope that he could still turn up alive.

That weekend, Pat and Georgina spent time exploring Manhattan together.

The weather was hot and humid, something that both of them were not accustomed to.

When they were walking through Central Park, they came across the lake in the centre of the park and hired out a small rowing boat.

They spent hours circling the lake; it probably reminded them of the lake near their home in the glen.

When they were back in Jackson Heights that evening, they begin the short walk from subway to their house. As they walk home, they are approached by an old lady. She begins whispering 'cocaine' a number of times. Taking Susan's advice, he keeps walking, putting his hand on Georgina's shoulder, looks down and nods to her to walk a little faster.

"I can't believe that old lady is selling drugs, Dad."

"How do you know she was selling drugs?"

"I'm not stupid, Dad. I heard Susan telling you about this place."

"Just be careful around here and will you please promise me that you will never take drugs?"

"I promise you, Dad, I will never take drugs," she says. "Now you have to make me a promise."

"What's that then?"

"Stop smoking," she says, and then pauses. "I'm only joking."

"Thank goodness for that then. I don't think I could keep that promise," he replies with a sigh of relief.

Back in their basement, Pat decides to call his sister Ann back in Donegal. He asks how things are at home and then talks to his mother, who seems happy to hear that he is working full-time. She then asks to talk to Georgina.

"Hello, Gran."

"Is that you, Georgina?"

"Yes, Gran, it's nice to hear your voice again."

"Well, it's great to hear your voice too, wee woman, everybody back here misses you terribly. Some of your school friends ask me after Mass on Sunday how you were doing and young Bosco here is lost without you."

"Tell Bosco I says hello."

They talk for over ten minutes; as Georgina puts down the phone, she begins to cry silently. Pat walks over and crouches down and hugs her and pats her on the back.

"I'm sorry for dragging you all the way over here," Pat says to Georgina, as he feels guilty about separating Georgina from her gran.

"Well, don't be, I love it over here, I'm only crying because I miss Gran."

"I thought you would hate me for bringing you all the way over here. It's just that I couldn't find any decent work back at home; if I could have, I would never have left."

Pat was so happy to hear Georgina say that. He had felt uneasy until then and was afraid she might have wanted to return home to Donegal, which he would have done, as he would do anything to make her happy.

As the weeks go by, they both settle in. Georgina makes a few new friends that live in the same block. Pat was left in charge of finishing the basement in the Poteen bar as the two Gallagher brothers had started new work in the city.

September arrives and Georgina is going to her new school in Woodside for the first time. Pat and Susan drive her and the child minder's daughter Maria there. They meet another Irish couple there, who have three children attending

St Sebastian School also. They introduce Georgina to their children; one of their girls is in Georgina's class.

Georgina settled into her new school and made lots of new friends. She would often reflect on her old school and how small the classrooms were. She felt proud that she had moved so far away from home and settled in a totally new environment. Often during classes, she would think of the friends she left behind and what they would think of her now.

It had been a long hot summer that year; luckily for Georgina and her father, their sallow skin never really burned that easily and they tanned easily. They were often mistaken to be of Italian descent.

On the first day of October, Marie calls the Poteen bar and asks for Tom. She received a call from the police that the remains of a body had been found in the lake at the back of the family holiday home in the Catskills. She was asked to come up and identify the body, as they believed that it was the body of her husband, Joe. Tom stood listening in shock as this was the news he had been dreading. He manages to come to terms with the fact that this may be Joe's body and arranges to go and meet her in Howard beach that day at three o'clock. As he puts down the phone, he makes his way to the toilets and is overcome with emotion. He locks himself in one of the cubicles and sits on the toilet with his hands covering his face. He then begins to cry uncontrollably.

He is in total shock from the news. He knew instinctively the day he was at that lake that Joe's body was in it somewhere.

Pat needed help moving seating and began shouting Tom's name down the corridor which led to the toilets. Tom doesn't answer, then stands up, grabs a handful of toilet tissue and wipes his tear-sodden face.

He walks upstairs to the main bar, and Pat tells him he had been looking for him everywhere as he needed his help.

"I've just heard some bad news, Pat. A body was found behind the Corbally family holiday home," Tom says, his voice weak and emotional.

"Do you know if it's Joe's?" Pat asks.

"He has still to be identified, but I know it's Joe's body," Tom says as he wipes a tear that was running down his cheek.

"I'm going to meet Maria at three o'clock. I think she wants me to go up and identify the body."

"I can go with you," Pat says, patting Tom on his back.

"Thanks, Pat. I could do with some company; I don't think I could do it on my own."

"Leave me back at the house and I'll pack a bag," Pat says. "You can pick me up on your way back from seeing Maria."

Tom calls his brother, who is working with a crew of plasterers in the Waldorf Astoria and breaks the news to him. Seamus isn't surprised by what he is told. He tells Tom that he can't leave the job, that he is working under a strict deadline to have his men out of the hotel by the end of the week

They lock up the bar and Tom drops Pat off at his apartment so he can prepare for the journey. Tom meets Maria at a coffee shop in Howard beach. She is very emotional and angry with her father as he would have sanctioned Joe's killing.

She feels totally responsible for allowing her brothers to take Joe to rehab, but she felt angry and embarrassed at Joe's lack of respect for her on her wedding day.

She didn't feel she could go through with identifying the body and asked if Tom could do it for her, which he agreed to do.

Georgina arrives home with her child minder outside their home.

"Hi, Daddy, why are you here?" Georgina asks as she gets out of Mrs Rodriguez's car.

"Hi, Georgina, and hello there, Mrs Rodriguez," Pat replies, avoiding giving an answer to Georgina question.

"You're home early today, Mr Boyle," Mrs Rodriguez asks. "Is everything OK?"

"Yes, I'm fine; I'm just heading off with my boss, Tom, for a day or two."

"Can I go with you?" Georgina asks.

"No, I'm sorry. I'll explain why some other time. I've talked to Susan. You can stay in her apartment until I get back. I hope you understand."

"Well, don't stay away too long, Look, there is your friend coming in that blue car," Georgina says after spotting Tom's car coming up their street.

Tom parks by the sidewalk and waves to Georgina. She smiles and waves back.

Pat kisses and hugs Georgina before he picks up a small bag of clothing.

"I'll call you later," he shouts back as he gets into Tom's car.

Tom rolls down his window and stops beside Georgina. He hands her a five-dollar bill and tells her to buy some candy for herself and Mrs Rodriguez's daughter.

Tom discusses with Pat that if this was Joe's body, he would make the arrangements for it to be taken back to be buried in Ireland and that he would travel back with it. Pat told him not to worry about finishing the bar and that he would look after everything until he gets back.

They reach the Catskills late that night and book into a motel for the night. Tom arranges with the police to meet the next day at the morgue.

Next day, they travel to the Corbally holiday home. When they get there, they both get out of the car and walk to the back of the house, towards the lake.

Because there had been no rain for over two months, the lake had receded and could be crossed on foot, it had dried up so much.

They then leave and go to the county morgue where two policemen were waiting for them.

They were shown a box of clothing that was removed from the body, also a wallet and Joe's driver licence. Tom asked did he have to see him; wasn't his licence enough proof that it was Joe, to which he was told that the body, or what was left of it, would have to be formally identified. Tom began to build up the courage to go into the next room, where the remains of Joe's body had been laid out on a stainless-steel table.

Tom, accompanied by the police officer, is led towards a door. There was a strong smell of rotten flesh as they enter the room next door. Tom gasps in horror as he looks at the skeletal remains that still had hair attached to the scalp, lying on the steel table. He stands frozen, unable to move. Pat can see him standing there and feels that he has to go in and support him. He walks towards the door; he then covers his nose with a tissue as the smell of death was overwhelming. He looks at the remains on the table; he couldn't tell if it was Joe's remains or not. The police officer asks Tom if Joe had any known features on his body that would help identify him. Tom was unable to answer him. The policeman then tells him he can leave the room as he can see how upset Tom has become. Pat persuades Tom to leave the room and walks him next door. He then goes back to talk to the policeman.

He tells him that Joe had two bottom teeth missing from a fight he had as a boxer when he was younger and part of his right index finger from a work-related accident.

They both walk for a closer look at the remains and can see that the two teeth were missing; also, part of the index finger was missing, just as Tom had said.

"It's Joe; I'm definite that it's Joe," Pat says with confidence.

"Thanks for your time; we can call this a positive identification then," the policeman says.

"I think you better get that other guy a stiff drink; he don't look too good."

"Can you tell if he was murdered? He was taken here by two men that have links with the Mafia," Pat asks.

"We will have confirmed first how he died and if he committed suicide. If we find any signs that he was murdered, there will have to be a full investigation and we would hope to find those responsible for this horrific crime."

Pat then makes his way out of the room. Tom is sitting on a small stool with his hands resting on each knee and staring blankly at the floor.

Pat puts a hand on Tom's shoulder and asks him if he is OK. Tom nods his head and stands up. Pat then tells him that they can go and would have to make arrangements with an undertaker to take Joe's body to New York to be waked.

The policeman reminds them that the body will not be released for a further two days. When they were outside the building, Pat tells Tom to go across the street for a drink, which Tom says that he needs badly.

The bar is an Irish-themed bar, with a sod of turf sitting on a shelf right in the centre of the back wall, with a sign above it saying, 'the old sod'. Tom drinks a few neat whiskeys and Pat just drinks two bottles as he says he would drive back. They then visit a funeral parlour and arrange for the body to be taken to a parlour in Woodside Queens. That night, Pat is back in Susan's apartment at 8.30 pm. Tom asks him to take the car with him. Georgina meets him on the street and smiles as he gets out.

"Is that your car, Dad?" Georgina says, hoping Pat will say the car is his.

"No, I'm sorry it's Tom's, my boss's car. He told me to take it with me tonight," he replies.

"Can we get a car of our own sometime?" she asks as they walk towards Susan's door.

"I'm going to buy a van and I'm going to have a big sign on the side of it saying Errigal Construction," Pat replies, as he had discussed sub-contracting work from Tom, and he would need a van to take tools and also materials to jobs.

Susan is surprised to see Pat so soon as she thought he would be another few days.

Pat asks Georgina if she could leave the room for five minutes because he has something private to discuss with Susan. Georgina already knows about Joe going missing and goes into Susan's bedroom while Pat talks to Susan. She keeps her ear to the door and can hear the conversation between them. She is shocked by what Pat is telling Susan. She can hear Susan crying when Pat tells her of the state that Joe's body was found in.

Later, Susan calls Georgina in for some supper before she goes to her bed.

That night, when she was in her basement bedroom sleeping, she is woken by Pat, who shouted out something in his sleep, in his room next door. She gets up, walks into Pat's room and as normal, Pat is snoring. She guessed that he may have had a nightmare about what he had seen when he saw Joe's body. That night, she heard him shout again but this time she hears him get up. He seems to walk into the kitchen and have a drink.

Next morning, Georgina tells Pat he was shouting in his sleep. He admits that he had a nightmare and he didn't want to talk about it.

A few days later, Joe's coffin arrives at the funeral parlour in Woodside. It was a huge shock for the Irish community in Queens. All his friends and drinking buddies go there and pay their respects.

Maria placed a framed picture of him that she had taken six months earlier. She sat close by his sealed coffin with Tom sitting by her side. Most people there had mixed emotions at the fact that she was there, as most of them knew that her brothers were the prime suspects in Joe's murder. Tom, on the other hand, knew that Maria was deeply in love with Joe and was hurting so much by what had happened. She had cut all ties with her family and vowed never to speak to them again. She even told the police that she believed that her family was responsible.

Maria takes Tom to one side. She tells him how frightened she is and is afraid of what could happen if she goes to Ireland with Joe's body. She thinks that close family members of Joe may not want her there and fears that she may be attacked by someone. Tom tries to reassure her that she is not to blame and that most people will sympathise with her. She tells Tom that only six months earlier, Joe was joking about if he was ever killed or died, he wanted to be buried beside his mum in Ireland.

She then tells Tom that she had made up her mind and would not travel to Ireland for the burial, but she would cover all costs involved.

They both sit telling stories about Joe. Tom tells how he was always jealous of him as he could have any girl he wanted, and he remembers the night that he first saw Maria; they were in Clancy's Bar in the city. Maria laughs and tells Tom she will never forget it because of the chat up line he used; it was really daft; she then laughs again.

"What was it?" Tom asks, smiling, "Or is it something rude?"

"No, I remember sitting at the bar with my good friend Julie; it was our first time in Clancy's. The next thing I remember was this guy standing at the bar beside me, about to order a drink. He turns around and looks at me, I smile. He then says in a slightly drunken voice, "How do you like your eggs in the morning?" I looked at my friend, she just shook her head, so I didn't answer him. Then he apologised and offered to buy me a drink. I looked into those piercing blue eyes, and he says, "How about a date?" That was the start of our relationship. I knew he loved to drink; he seemed to handle it well, and at the beginning, it didn't bother me. I told him I wasn't happy about it, and my family was asking questions about his drinking. We argued a lot about it. He let me down so many times. I was about to finish with him over a year ago. But then he promised that he would cut down on it and stop drinking after we married but in the few months before the wedding, he seemed to be drinking more and more," Maria says.

"I noticed lately that he seemed to be slurring his words. This would be in the second half of the day when he should be sobering up," Tom says. "But a few weeks ago, I found an empty whiskey bottle in a tool belt. I knew he had to be drinking on the quiet."

Tom shared some more stories with Maria about growing up with Joe back in Letterkenny before Maria leaves in a taxi. Tom tells her that he will call her from Ireland after Joe's burial at Conwal cemetery as she gets into the taxi.

The body arrives three days later at St Eunan's Cathedral Letterkenny. It reposes there overnight for ten o'clock Mass next morning. That morning, over three hundred friends and relations pack into the cathedral. The priest talks of the tough upbringing that Joe endured and thanks the Gallagher family for taking him into their home as one of their own. It rains heavily during the burial, but everyone felt it was their duty to be there for this young man, who was taken in the prime of his life.

Maria had given Tom a thousand dollars to pay for a meal in Gallagher's Hotel, to which he invites all of Joe's close friends. Most of them can't believe that he was murdered. For people in this small town like Letterkenny, this was unheard of.

Tom spends an extra week in Letterkenny. He also travels to Pat's sister's house in the Poisoned Glen. He had taken back a few small presents and photos that Georgina wanted to give her gran. Old grandma Boyle is so pleased to meet Tom and to know that her grown up son is doing so well. Tom had never climbed Errigal before and always wanted to do it, so Mick Kelly goes with him to show him the way.

At the top of the mountain, Tom looks at the beauty of the countryside around him. His thoughts turn to Pat and Georgina, who had to leave this beautiful place, and how hard it must have been for Pat at 35 years old.

Back in New York, Pat buys a second-hand Ford transit, short wheel base van. He keeps it a secret from Georgina, so he can get the name painted on the side.

A week later, Georgina is playing next door with the child minder's daughter when a black Transit pulls up and parks on the sidewalk. At first, Georgina doesn't pay attention to it, then the name on the side catches her attention. She reads the name in disbelief; it reads, Errigal Construction New York. Then she thinks, that can't be, so she looks at the driver, and to her joy, it is her father, sitting there as proud as punch with a smile from ear to ear, watching Georgina's reaction.

"When did you get this, Dad?" Georgina asks, walking quickly alongside the van.

"I bought it last week, and I had the name put on it during the week."

"Can I go for a ride in it?"

"Sure, hop in."

Georgina runs into the child minder's home and tells her that she is going with her father for a run in his new van. Mrs Rodriguez comes out to see Pat and asks can her daughter go for the run, which Pat agrees to.

Pat drives up to Sunnyside and back towards the deli in front of the Poteen Bar. Pat takes the two young girls in and buys them ice cream cones. The old Chinese guy begins to recognise Pat as a regular in his shop. He always enjoys a laugh, a joke with him. Pat then walks across the street, taking the two girls with him; they go into the Irish import shop. He was in looking for a few Irish cassette tapes. One of the tapes he was looking for by the Wolfe Tones wasn't in stock so Mick told him he would order it for him. There were a few guys sitting at the bar having a drink; the next minute, a fight breaks out between two of them. Mick's father comes out from behind the bar. He tries to pull one of the men back as he punched and kicked the other who was curled up on the floor. But to his shock, he turns around and punches old John in the face, knocking him on to his back. Mick runs to his father and shouts at the man to stop. The man shouts back in a strong Dublin accent that he will get the same if he doesn't shut up.

This only enrages Mick who tells him that he is only a scumbag for hitting his old man. Pat tells Georgina and the other young girl to stay in the shop as he wanted to help out. Pat walks up to the man. He tells him to get out or he would put him out on his head. The man looks at Pat and sizes him up. Pat, who stood over six-foot tall, looks down at him, repeats for him to get out, only this time he raises his voice and points at the door. Georgina watches as the man walks slowly towards the door followed by her father. Pat then locks the door and helps old John to his feet; as he sits down, Mick is concerned for him. He reassures them that he is OK, and he tells them that the guy punches like a girl, which brings a smile to their faces. The other guy was lying in the corner. Pat goes over; the man is bleeding from a cut above his left eye. Pat asks him if he wants an ambulance, to which he replies 'No'. Pat helps him to his feet, and he then sits up at the bar again. Old John asks who the other guy was. The man tells him he didn't know the guy; that he caught him taking some of his money from the bar, "The next thing I knew he was punching and kicking me." Old John tells him to get washed up, and he would put him up a few free drinks. All of them thank Pat for helping out. Mick tells him if they ever need a doorman, he gets the job.

Pat didn't like the idea that Georgina witnessed any of this, and he tells them that they will go back home again.

It's only a short distance back to the apartment, but Georgina and her little friend keep throwing lots of questions at him about what happened in the bar. Pat feels uncomfortable about some of the questions and tries unsuccessfully to change the subject.

Back at the house, Pat drives his van up towards Susan's garage and begins work on shelving the van. He gives Georgina some lessons on how to cut wood. She loves this; even though she is only twelve years old, she can handle the saw as good as any adult. As Pat watches her cutting, he can see a lot of himself in her. He thinks back to when his own father would let him get involved in carpentry work around the farm. He also had natural ability for using saws and chisels belonging to his father. That evening just after nine, Susan arrives home. She sees the van for the first time as she walks up her drive and tells Pat how great it looks. Georgina sits in the driver's seat and blows the horn.

Susan walks from the back to the front of the van to see who did it.

"It's you," says Susan. "You gave me a fright; I wasn't expecting that."

"Do you like the name on the van?" Georgina asks.

"Oh, yes," Susan says. "But do you think anybody in New York will have a clue what Errigal means?"

"I don't care what they think; I like it and my dad likes it."

"Susan!" Pat shouts from the back of the van. "I'll be promoting the most beautiful place in the world on my van. The Irish tourism board should be giving me commission."

"Ah, I'm sure they will, and pigs will fly," says Susan. "I see you'll have a little helper very soon."

"You're right there," Pat replies. "You should see the way that wee girl can handle a saw; she would put a few men I know to shame."

"Good for you, Georgina," Susan says, "I still have a few little jobs for you two to sort out yet. What about tomorrow, it's Saturday; are you working anywhere?"

"I want to go back to the Bronx zoo again," Georgina says eagerly. "Dad, don't you remember you said you would take me this weekend?"

"You're right, I completely forgot about it," Pat says in an apologetic manner. "We will go, and to tell you what, I'm looking forward to it; I've never been to a zoo before."

"Well, you're in for a treat," says Susan. "The Bronx zoo is one of the best zoos in the world."

Susan orders a Chinese takeaway for them. They all eat it down in the basement. Georgina and Pat have beef with broccoli and pork fried rice. Susan has vegetable chow mein and takes down some iced tea from her apartment for them to drink.

Next morning, they all have breakfast in Susan's apartment. Georgina has taken a liking to eating syrup and pancakes for breakfast; Pat, on the other hand, sticks to his usual scrambled eggs on toast. Georgina tells them how life has changed so much for her and how she loves going to her new school.

Susan offers to take her car that morning, but Georgina insists that they take the subway; in the end, Georgina wins the vote. Pat tells them he is looking forward to seeing the monkeys, as they take the number seven line to the city.

They then change and take a train northbound towards the Bronx. Pat felt uncomfortable, as they were the only white people on the carriage, but the closer they get to the zoo the more the carriage empties. The train stops at 170 Street Station, one stop away from the zoo. A lot of the passengers get off at this stop, leaving only a black man reading a newspaper and what looks like his two children each side of him and another black youth on Pat's right hand side. The doors close, then the train begins to move off slowly. Pat, as he sits next to Georgina, hears a little crackling sound through the noise of the train moving off. He can't figure out what it is. He looks up the carriage and keeps hearing the sound at two-second intervals.

Then suddenly, he notices a sprinkling of glass fall from the window onto the plastic seat; he then sees it happen again, then again. He looks to the other side of the carriage and realises that bullets are going from one side window through the opposite side and it's getting closer to them.

"Get down everyone," Pat shouts as he grabs Georgina and pulls her to the floor.

"What is wrong with you, Dad, why are you doing this?" Georgina says as her father pins her to the floor of the train.

"Get down, Susan, there's someone shooting at the train," shouts Pat.

"There is no one shooting at the train, Pat, have you gone crazy?" Susan says.

Pat doesn't hesitate, he gets up on his knees and grabs Susan by the shoulders and pulls her on to the floor, shouting 'get down' and repeating it over and over.

"What is wrong with you Pat?" Susan says, bewildered by his actions.

"Look at the windows," Pat shouts, pointing as another bullet passes silently through the glass; any sound that was there is drowned out by the sound of the train moving off.

Susan then realises what Pat was seeing and she then shouts to the man on Pat's right to get down, just as he realises himself what is happening and ducks down to the floor.

They all shout at the man with the two kids to get down. He looks over his newspaper through a pair of reading glasses for a moment, just shakes his head and begins reading his paper again. The two children are sitting on their knees looking out the window with their backs facing the centre of the carriage, not paying attention to anyone lying on the floor. To all of them lying on the floor, they can only watch helplessly as the bullets pass beside the first child and luckily past the second child.

They lie on the floor until they are well out of the station. The man lying on the floor next to them then gets up on his knees and looks out. He then stands up and slides open the top pane of the glass. He shouts out, 'You dumb motherfucker' to the person doing the shooting. Pat feels it is safe enough for them to sit down again and asks the man next to him if he knew who did it. But the man just shook his head saying no. They stand in the centre of the carriage in shock at what happened. Pat points out that there is a bullet hole about every three feet. Georgina revels in the moment. She smiles and feels excited by what happened, unlike her aunt who is still shaking uncontrollably.

"Are you OK?" Georgina asks Susan, as she notices her still shaking.

"No, I can't believe what happened to us, we could have been killed. What sort of maniac was shooting like that?" says Susan, her voice etched with anger.

"I wonder if anyone was hit in the other carriages, or were we the only carriage to be shot at?"

The train begins to slow down as it nears the next stop at the zoo. Pat says that the cops will probably be waiting to question everyone when they get off.

When it stops and they get out, they look along the side of the train.

Almost every window had been shot at, and then, as if nothing happened, the doors close and the train moves off.

"I can't believe it," Pat says holding his hand up in the air with open palms. "Is that normal here?"

"I've been living in this city a long time now and by God, I have never seen anything like that before," Susan replies.

"I can't believe that the train just drove off as if nothing happened," Pat says. "I wonder will there be any cops downstairs or near the zoo, we would need to report this."

They walk down the steps on to the street but can't see any cops. Pat looks up a side street; again, he can't see any cops. They then decide that there is no point in them worrying about it if no one else is, so they go into the zoo.

Pat, who had never been to a zoo before, really enjoys seeing the different types of wild creatures. They spend almost an hour watching the monkeys as they climb trees and as males seemed to fight for dominance of their group. Pat tells Georgina that he could spend all day watching them as he thinks everything they do is so comical.

During their visit, they never thought once about the shooting incident that happened on the way there. But as they make their way back to the train, it all comes flooding back to them. Susan asks if they want to take a taxi back as she is still afraid and full of anxiety. She just can't get out of her head how close they had come to being killed.

Pat tries to reassure Susan that the chances of the same thing happening on the way back are very slim, but Susan seems to be nervous so Pat waves down a yellow cab.

Back at Susan's apartment that evening, while all three of them were watching the news, as Pat was convinced that the shooting would be mentioned, a knock came to the door. Susan gets up from her blue reclining chair.

"Hi there, Tom, when did you get back?" asks Susan.

"I'm just back; this is my first stop," he replies. "Is the big man in? I was knocking on the basement door but there was no one in."

"He sure is, come on in, and I'll get you a coffee; you must be jet lagged."

"Hi there, big man and hello, Georgie, your gran gave me something for you," Tom says, holding a box about one-foot square.

"What is it?" Georgina says hopping up from the sofa and reaching for the box.

"I haven't a clue, open it and find out," he replies.

"Here, Pat, she sent this over to you too," Tom says as he pulls a small bag out of his pocket.

Georgina rips open the box. She looks inside and sees something wrapped in newspaper inside. She takes it out and unwraps it.

"It's my old teddy; I had forgotten to take it with me. What did you get, Dad?"

"My old pipe and a packet of tobacco," he says. "The only thing is I didn't forget it, I was trying to give it up by coming over here, but by God am I glad to see it again."

"Well, you're not smoking it in here; you can take it outside to the bench at the front."

"Jesus, you sound just like your sister Annie back at home. Come on outside with me, Tom, so I can get this baby lit up again."

"Tom, I'll bring your coffee out to you, or would you two prefer a cool beer?"

"I'd love a nice cool beer, Susan. It's so humid here after spending time back in the home country."

"Pat, you haven't stopped smiling since I gave you that pipe," Tom says as he sits on the bench beside Pat.

"Just you wait till I get this old chimney smoking again, it's pure heaven," he replies.

Pat then fills the pipe and packs it down with his finger. He then takes out matches, then lights it up, pulling and puffing with a contented look upon his face.

Susan takes them out a bottle of Budweiser each and a few sandwiches.

Tom tells Pat all about Joe's funeral and how big the crowd was that turned up at St Eunan's Cathedral the morning of his burial.

Susan and Georgina take out two fold-up chairs to sit on.

"Dad, are you going to show Tom your new van?"

"To tell you the truth, I had forgotten all about it; stay sitting there, Tom, I'll get it out of the garage."

Pat opens Susan's garage door and parks his van on the street in front of Susan's house, so that Tom could get a proper view of it.

"My God, Pat, you're only in the country over six months and you're way ahead of me already. I'll probably end up working for you next," Tom says as he gets up to have a closer look at the van. "I love the name, just wait till you have a fleet of them on the road."

"I'll be lucky if I can keep this one on the road," Tom says as he gets out and walks towards the rear of the van, "Have a look in the back; I shelved it."

Tom walks up through the back of the van and admires the way Pat has laid out the shelving for holding tools and screws and nails.

Pat stands at the back smoking his pipe, pointing and explaining what some of the empty shelves are intended for. Georgina tells Tom that she had helped her father to cut some of the shelves. Tom gets out; he then has a better look at the lettering and rubs his fingers across it.

They go back to the bench and finish off their beer. Susan then begins to tell Tom about what happened to them as they travelled on the train that morning.

She tells him that they could have been killed so easily only for Pat's quick reaction.

"That's one thing I have, is a pair of good ears," Pat says, proud that he had probably saved their lives.

"You're all very lucky then," Tom says, shocked by what Susan had told him, "I never heard of that happening before, but it can be dangerous up there, I wouldn't travel up there at night, it would be risky."

"Well, I won't be travelling there by train anymore," Susan says in a stern voice.

"It didn't scare me," Georgina says. "I found it exciting; it was if I was in a movie."

"You're a brave little girl; most children of your age would be scared out of their wits if that happened to them," Tom says.

"Yeah, Tom," Susan says. "She is very brave; did you ever see a little girl settle in so well? You would think she grew up here."

Georgina stands there listening to all the compliments with a smile on her face. But with that, she looks down at her teddy and strong memories come flooding back.

Her thoughts wander to how her gran would always tuck her in at night by praying to her mother. Georgina would hold the bears and paws together, as if it were praying too.

Then Gran would always kiss both of them goodnight before turning off the light.

The little girl next door, Vanessa, says hello to everyone and comes over to see Georgina.

Georgina shows her teddy to Vanessa. She then hands it to her, telling her that her mother had bought it for her after she was born and how her Gran had sent it over with Tom.

Vanessa smiles as she holds the teddy; she understands how much it means to Georgina. Then Vanessa invites Georgina over to her house for a sleepover.

She asks her father if it was OK, without any hesitation; he smiles and then tells her to go fetch her toothbrush and pyjamas. She rushes to the basement to fetch her nightclothes and wishes everyone good night before she leaves, taking her beloved teddy with her.

On the street, a gang of youths passing by on the street, one of them wearing a red and white bandana, stops outside the gate. He looks at Pat for a moment.

"Have you got a spare cigarette, old man?" he says to Pat in an intimidating manner.

Pat, who was puffing on his pipe, turns his head and looks at Tom in disbelief.

Pat thinks about what he had just said; he took great offence about being told that he was an old man.

"Sorry, young man, but I don't smoke cigarettes, they're very bad for your health," Pat says with sarcasm, in revenge for calling him an old man.

A few of the youths begin laughing at Pat's remark. The young guy pushes the gate open in anger so hard it slams against the side fence and rebounds against his knees.

He jumps back grabbing his knee and begins to limp off in shame as the laughter gets louder.

"What an idiot. If he had said it nicely, I might have given him one but the cheek of him to call me old," Pat says.

"God, Pat, have you looked in the mirror lately?" Susan asks, "There's quite a few grey hairs there now but you still look OK; what do you think Tom?"

"Ah, he has a few years left in him yet," Tom says as he punches Pat playfully on his shoulder.

Tom then stands up and stretches his arms and says, "I'd better be getting back home. I could do with a good night's sleep. Are you coming for the big St Patrick's Day party in the Poteen and the official opening of the new party room tomorrow, Pat?

"We're all going down for the opening, I've a few things to tidy up there, but I'll finish them off on Monday when things have quietened down," Pat says.

Next morning, the Boyles all walk to Mass at St Sebastian's in Woodside. On the way there, almost everyone they meet is dressed in green.

The weather is beautiful that morning. After Mass, Pat treats them all to a meal at the Steakhouse, and after the meal, they take the subway back to Jackson Heights and then make their way to the Poteen bar.

A large crowd of Irish people have already gathered in the first floor of the bar, with a green ribbon across the steps leading to the basement.

In the basement, a three-piece band are setting up on the stage area. Tom and his brother, Seamus, are helping out moving tables for food. Little Mike is dressed in a large green hat and jacket; he was also wearing a false beard.

"You look like a leprechaun, Mick," Georgina says, smiling.

"I dress like this every St Patrick's day; everybody loves it, especially young kids like you."

"Come here, Mick, and I'll pin some shamrocks on your collar. I grew these in my window ledge," Susan says, then pins them on his jacket. "This is my first year to miss the parade in the city."

"I haven't been to the parade myself in ten years; this is our busiest day of the year," Mick tells Susan. "I have just found out that one of the Clancy Brothers I booked to perform the opening ceremony is unable to attend."

"Who will do it at this short notice?" Susan asks.

"I just don't know," he replies.

He can't think of anyone who can replace him. He asks Tom if he could think of anyone, but he just stands there shaking his head. He goes upstairs and can see little Georgina standing with her father at the bar. He thinks about it for a moment and says to himself that she would be perfect.

He walks towards Pat, then stops about four feet away; he then waves to him and calls him over. He tells Pat about his predicament and asks Pat if he would mind if Georgina would cut the tape for the opening ceremony. Pat told him it would be an honour, and then he asks Georgina if she would do it. Georgina is overwhelmed and just replies, "Yes." She can't think why she has been chosen. She feels she did not deserve to do it and stands there with a look of disbelief. Her aunt Susan congratulates her, as Mick tells her what he wants her to do.

"Ladies and gentlemen, I am sorry but none of the Clancy Brothers could make it for the opening," Mick says. "But I have an even better replacement to do the grand opening, a cute little Irish girl all the way from dear old Donegal. Let me introduce you all to miss Georgina Boyle."

Everyone cheers and claps as Georgina smiles as she makes her way to the stairs. Mick then hands her a large pair of scissors, then tells the crowd that he can't call it the Clancy Room, and he was going to leave it up to Georgina to give it a name. Georgina stands there thinking for a few moments, her mind blank, then she sees her father looking at her, mouthing words with no sound. He did it a few times, but no one could see him. She recognises that he is saying Errigal, so she says timidly to Mick, "Errigal," as she looks for the crowd's reaction to the name.

"Errigal it is then," shouts Mick.

"Yes," shouts Pat as he throws a fist in the air.

"You can cut the ribbon now, Georgie," Mick says.

Georgina opens the large scissors and begins to cut the green ribbon; then as it is cut in two, there is a large cheer and whistle from the crowd.

Everyone claps as Mick declares that their new party room, which will be officially called the Errigal Room, is now open.

Mick takes Georgina by the hand when a few of the crowd tell them to wait for a few photos; they stand and smile. Georgina never had so much attention in her life and is really enjoying it. Then Mick tells Georgina to lead the way as everyone follows them to the basement, cheering as they do.

Pat and Susan follow in the crowd, so proud of Georgina being picked to cut the ribbon in the opening ceremony. The band begins playing as the crowd packs the large oak panelled room. Pat meets up with the two Gallagher brothers for a few beers.

Mick gets everyone in the mood by performing one of his silly dances that he had conjured up. He invites Georgina who is caught in the moment to join him. To Pat's surprise, she accepts, and Mick tells her to copy everything he does. Georgina begins copying his moves as a few others join in dancing.

Mick's father arrives and gives a few free drinks to Pat and the Gallaghers. Susan joins Georgina dancing with all the other partygoers. Susan had never seen Georgina so happy and stayed out on the floor dancing until Georgina eventually got tired.

At eleven thirty, Susan persuades Pat to go home, but as he begins to stand up, he staggers and needs help to stand on his feet. Tom helps him until he is outside the bar, then Susan flags down a cab to take them home.

Both girls help Pat by standing on each side of him and holding on to his arms and leading him down the basement steps.

He just plonks down on his bed and almost immediately falls asleep.

Susan closes his door and then puts on the whistling kettle for a cup tea.

"I hate it when Dad gets drunk like he did tonight," Georgina says with a frown. "And he always snores louder when he has drink in him."

"I think he has already started, just listen," Susan says as she hears Pat's snoring getting louder.

"You poor girl, how will you sleep with that racket next door to you?"

"I'm used to it now, but sometimes I put tissue in my ears; I think I'll have to do just that tonight," she says with a sigh.

"You know we were so proud of you tonight, and by the way, had you any other name other than the one your father forced upon you?"

"No, my mind was completely blank. I wasn't expecting that I would have to name it, but I do like the idea that it is called the Errigal Room.

"Yea, I like it myself. I'm going to call your gran, and you can tell her all about it."

Susan calls her sister Mary, and Bosco answers the phone. Susan talks to him for a few minutes then hands the phone to Georgina.

It's the first time that they have talked to each other since she had left Ireland.

Georgina had so much to tell him about her new life and was eager to find out what her old school friends were up to.

Bosco told her that as soon as he turned seventeen that he would go and live in New York too; Georgina is so happy to hear him say this as Bosco was one of her very best friends.

Gran, who is in the same room as Bosco, asks him to let her have the phone so that she can talk to Georgina.

Georgina tells her gran about the great day she had, and that she was asked to cut the ribbon at the opening of the new room, which her father was involved in building.

Gran listens intently. She feels a great longing to be close to Georgina and misses her company so much, it's almost unbearable. But listening to her voice and knowing that her son and granddaughter are doing so well makes it a worthy sacrifice.

Susan sits quietly beside Georgina drinking her coffee. She eavesdrops on the conversation. She is anxious to talk to her mother and whispers to Georgina for Gran to stay on the line as she wanted to talk to her.

Eventually, Georgina hands the phone to her. Gran tells her that she hasn't been feeling the best lately and is always very tired. Susan advises her that she should go to her doctor, but Gran had never been to a doctor in her life. The only time she would visit one was when her own children were ill. Susan then talks to her sister. Mary tells Susan that she had tried on a few occasions to persuade her mother to visit a doctor, but she would always refuse. Susan tells Mary that she should try her very best to get her to a doctor and that she would try and fly home for Christmas.

That Christmas, as soon as Georgina got her school holidays, they all fly back home.

They are welcomed home with open arms. Georgina and Gran were inseparable that first night with Georgina sitting on her grandma's lap talking nonstop about New York, her gran just sits listening, looking closely at Georgina's face, which was bathed in innocence, sometimes not taking on board anything Georgina is saying but smiles, holding her arms around her precious granddaughter.

It was a tight squeeze in the Kelly home, with three others staying there, but the old home place would be too damp and cold.

Early one morning, Mary and Susan decided that they will confront their mother about her failing health. They get her up for breakfast, but walking in the room towards the table, she looked stiff and slow, taking small steps.

"How are we this morning, mother?" Susan says, while sitting beside her sister, both of them drinking tea.

"Oh, I've been better, but that's old age for you," Gran replies, holding on to the table as she eases herself slowly on to the chair at the top of the table.

"You know, you've slowed down a lot more, Mammy, in the past few months. We think you should go for a check-up. Will you please go for us?" Mary says, pleading with her mother.

"I'll be 71 years old in three weeks' time, and in all that time, I've never had to visit a doctor; at this stage of my life, whatever is for me, is for me, as my own mother used to say," Gran says.

"Anyway, Mum, will you have a bowl of porridge and a wee cup of tea?" Susan says, changing the subject.

"Ah, I will, I've been spoilt since I moved here, Mary won't let me dip a finger."

Both her daughters are afraid to overstep the mark. They realise that Gran has no intention of visiting the doctor, no matter how much they persist.

Susan had come home with the intention of forcing her mother into seeing a doctor; she now had to accept it would be impossible. Her mother was set in her ways and would never change. Susan, as much as she didn't like to admit it, admired her mother's strong willpower.

After a week's stay in Donegal, they then fly back to New York; it broke their hearts having to leave but knew that time would heal their heartache. The weather was bitter cold with heavy snowfall; almost a foot of snow had fallen.

Ms Green, a retired nurse, who rents the top floor, was back in New York for the Christmas holidays.

She meets Pat and Georgina for the first time. She had moved to New York back in the fifties. After she retired, she sold her house in New York and had bought an apartment in Florida.

Christmas would not be Christmas if she did not spend it in New York.

She invited the Boyles to her apartment for New Year's Day for a meal.

Life had changed so much for Pat and Georgina; they had embraced New York and made it their home. Georgina has enjoyed every moment of her new life and her father, who had struggled to find any sort of work back in Ireland, is now working full-time and his earnings are four times what he would earn at home.

With the bitter cold that January, Pat was lucky enough that he was working inside at a job down on Canal Street in the city. Tom began to expand his business, making Pat a foreman. Pat was to learn of the Mafia control of the construction industries in the city.

They had almost total control of the Concrete Union and one who crossed them could find themselves buried in concrete. The commission is a governing body of the Mafia in the United States. Although its makeup has changed several times since its 1931 creation, the bosses of the New York Five Families still provide the core membership of The Commission. The predecessor organisation was the National Crime Syndicate which was a national alliance with many organised crime figures.

New York Concrete District Workers Council's union leader represented thousands of labourers needed for constructing foundations, walls and floors, the guts of every high-rise commercial and residential building in Manhattan, thus his importance as the overseer of the Commission's 'Concrete Club' and the Five Families' other construction rackets.

The Italians were not the only nationality to be involved in extortion in New York; the Irish gangsters from the early sixties were involved in racketeering and extortion. They were better known as the Westies and were based in what was known as Hell's Kitchen. Black African Americans were also involved in extorting money from construction workers who carried out work in what would be regarded as their turf. Also, there were many Hispanic gangs involved in racketeering.

One of the best organised and most violent in New York were the Latin Kings who were involved in many brutal murders.

All of these groups controlled different sections of the five boroughs of New York. Pat's first encounter with one of these groups was when he began subcontracting the building of a church for Tom in Far Rockaway, Queens.

It was Pat's third year in New York; he had built a good reputation as a building contractor and had another young guy, who had just emigrated, working for him full-time. Tom had begun advertising in the Yellow Pages and because of that, always had surplus work that he would pass on to people he trusted, such as Pat.

He had priced building a church in Far Rockaway and was awarded the contract. The only problem was that he was too busy to do the job himself, so he asked Pat if he was interested in subcontracting from him. Pat was interested, so he and Tom went down to look at it. When they get there and drive through the main street, they notice how run down the area has become. They notice all the Irish-named buildings but not a single white person on the street. Tom feels uneasy at the thought of Pat working in the area and questions Pat on his views on working in the area. Pat explains to Tom that he's up for the challenge and is looking forward to getting started.

When they get to the site where the church is to be erected, Pastor Jacob and his church assistant called Moses are sitting in a school bus outside the gate.

Tom explains before they get out of his van that Jacob drives the bus as a full-time job, but Pat can't stop laughing, telling Tom that he would like to see their local priest back in Ireland driving a school bus.

Tom introduces the men to Pat and explains how he will be in charge of building their new church. Pastor Jacob explains that his assistant, Moses, will supply all the materials that were needed and that they would have the plumbing and electrics done by other contractors. He also advises Pat not to work in the area after dark and that a local gang in the area controls a lot of what happens there.

Pat tells them that he will make a start a week later and gives a list of material that are needed for the first stage.

Georgina, now fourteen years old, is well known by the young gangs that patrol the Jackson Heights area. Although she is never involved with any of the gangs, she is very friendly with one boy in particular, Adam Lopes, who is in her class at high school.

Both of them want to join the army when they leave school and have a keen interest in collecting the magazine, *Soldier of Fortune*. They quiz each other regularly on their knowledge of the different types of guns and ammunition. He trusts Georgina more than he trusts the members of the gang and confides in her his feelings about his drug-dealing father and how his mother had abandoned him when he was only four years old. One day, Susan gets a knock at the door; as she opens it, a young man stands there wearing a denim jacket with the sleeves cut from it.

"Hi, is Georgie here? I'm Adam. I knocked on the basement door but no one answered."

"Yea, she's here, I'm her Aunt Susan. Georgina!" Susan shouts, "Can you come to the door?"

Georgina already hearing Adam's voice from the kitchen comes running to the door.

"Hi, Adam," Georgina says, "I'm going out for a while; tell Dad I'll see him later."

They begin walking towards the subway when Adam stops walking and is anxious to tell Georgina something that is on his mind.

"Georgie, I've found something, but I don't think I can show what I've found."

"Come on, Adam, you can't just tell me that then expect me not to ask you what you've found."

"Georgie, it's difficult; I know I can trust you, but I could be putting your life in danger by showing you it."

"What is it, is it a thing or is it a body, or is it drugs? You've made me so curious I won't stop asking until you tell me what it is."

Adam just stands there, his eyes looking upwards; his thoughts were trying to choose the right words without giving too much away. He decides then not to give her too much information there and then.

"I'm going to show you something, but you'll have to promise on your life never to tell anyone what I'm about to show you."

"I swear on my life, I will tell no one about whatever it is you are going to show me. Come on, you know you can trust me."

"OK then, we've got to walk back to my house."

"Aren't you going to tell me what it is?"

"No, all will be revealed when we get there."

They then walk the two blocks to Adam's home. On the way, Adam explains that his father had gone to South America on business and he was left to fend for himself.

Adam takes the steps down to the basement at his home and then pulls out a set of keys from his pocket.

Georgina notices that the door is made of metal and the side windows are bricked up.

Adam begins to unlock a series of three locks that are spaced along the edge of the door. Even this looks strange to Georgina, and she wonders what was so important that this basement had to be so secure.

Adam pushes open the heavy metal door and walks in, switches on the light. He tells Georgina to come in quickly. He then closes the door, sliding two large bolts across and locks the door from the inside.

"Last night was my first time in here," Adam explains. "My father never would allow me down here. So I checked out his bedroom and found the keys hidden in the back of a drawer. I always used to wonder what he was hiding here. Sometimes, groups of men would come here. It sounded as if there was a big party going on, with loud music playing. It used to bug me why I wasn't invited, now I know why."

"What is it? There's nothing special here," Georgina says as she looks up and down the room.

There's a small bar at the far end of the room and some chairs and a table. Well, there is also that large picture of Elvis on the opposite side of the room.

"So tell me, what is the big secret?"

"Help me move these chairs and tables, so we can roll up this rug," Adam says.

Georgina and Adam move all the chairs to the side of the room, and then they roll up the large rug. As they do, it reveals two large metal doors with small holes where fingers could fit as a grip to open them. They manage to pull open both doors, and then Adam begins to walk down a set of steps into what seems to look like a dark hole. He then uses a lighter he had in his pocket and strikes it a few times until it lights up. He looks around on a wall on his left and finds a switch and turns the light on.

"Come down here, Georgie," he shouts.

"What is this place?" Georgina says as she walks down the steps. "Wow, look at all those guns; there must be a thousand of them. What does he need all these for?"

In the room, which was about half the size of the room above, were over a thousand different types of rifles and pistols. They were housed carefully in different cabinets with their ammunition for each one in drawers below.

Georgina walks slowly, with her mouth ajar, looking at all the different types of guns on display.

"I'm gobsmacked. Where did your dad get all these guns?" she asks; her voice full of excitement."

"I don't know, but it scares me to think what they might be used for. I think my dad is some kind of illegal dealer."

Adam opens one of the cabinets and takes out a 10/22 Ruger rifle with suppressor attached and then hands it to Georgina. He then takes out one for himself and takes two ten-round magazine clips from the drawer below. Both he and Georgina know everything about this hunting rifle, but it's their very first time to hold one in their hands.

"I expected it to be a lot heavier," Georgina says as she tries to gauge the weight of the rifle.

"It must weigh five or six pounds. My dad's .22 back in Ireland was heavier."

"Follow me, Georgie, up the steps and take your clip, it's got ten rounds in it."

"Why, we can't use them up there, Adam, and I'm not taking it out outside."

"Just follow me; I've got one more surprise for you."

Adam walks towards the large six-foot picture of Elvis. He tells Georgina that his father is a big fan of his, then grips the edge of the frame and gives it a tug.

The picture opens out into the room, like a door to reveal another steel door behind it. Adam smiles at Georgina's reaction as he does so. He then gets out the keys from his pocket and unlocks the door, which opens into a hidden room.

He reaches around the doorframe and switches the lights on, then they both walk in.

The room is only about five feet wide but is the full length of the basement, which is about fifty feet long. The wall and ceiling are covered in soundproofing, with a lot of sand bags piled up to the ceiling at the opposite side of the room.

Adam shows Georgina a switch on the wall. He presses it and a paper target comes towards them on a rail attached to the ceiling.

"This place is unbelievable, Adam, have you tried shooting yet?"

"No, not yet. It was kind of scary when I first discovered it. I just rushed through every place quickly, then I thought about you, and I wished that you were with me."

"Ah, you're so kind," Georgina says, putting one arm around Adam, giving him a hug.

She is holding the rifle in the other hand and still has her arm around Adam, then looks into his eyes. She sees he looks a little embarrassed, so she gives him a kiss on his cheek.

"Do you know how to load the clip?" he says, feeling slightly embarrassed after being kissed by Georgina. He then demonstrates on his gun and attaches the clip.

"That looks simple," she replies, as she attaches her clip. "You go first."

"Not until I do something first," he replies, walking towards the small bar in the room next door. He then puts in a cassette tape of the rock band, Led Zeppelin and turns up the volume full blast. The room has four large speakers and the sound thunders through the room. Both of them run towards the shooting chamber and close the door behind them. The sound of the music is almost completely drowned out by the soundproofing.

"What is that all about, Adam?"

"That's what my father would do. I used to think that he was having a big party down here, and never inviting me, but it was to stop anyone hearing the gunshots. I have to admit, I never heard one shot, even though I was just above them."

"I have to say, I'm really impressed, Adam, but let's put this away, start shooting."

"OK then," he replies as he presses the button for the paper target to return to the opposite side of the room. Georgina watches as he takes aim. She realises he doesn't have the butt of the rifle tight against his shoulder, but before she could say anything, he fires the gun and seems to have hurt his shoulder.

"Are you OK?" Georgina asks, concerned that Adam may have damaged his shoulder.

"I'm fine," he then presses the button for the paper target to return.

The target stops in front of them, totally intact, with no visible signs of a bullet being shot through it.

"Let me show you how my father taught me back at home. Are you watching me?" she says aggressively as she lifts the rifle up. "Press the button for the target, please."

Georgina waits as the paper target returns to the opposite side of the long narrow room. She then holds the gun tight against her shoulder. She then crouches her legs in a forward motion, sitting tight, she aims and fires, then another four times in a row.

Adam feels a little insecure that he doesn't know how to use the gun as good as Georgina.

Georgina presses the button and the target begins to come towards her.

"Aha, I did it, I did it. I got all five and look, two of them are in the centre ring. I am so happy," Georgina says, as she hops up and down in excitement.

"Stand back; let me show you how it should be done, Georgie boy. Hey, put on a new target on the track for me," he says full of enthusiasm, but dreading the chance that he would make the same mistake again. He then lifts his gun and places the butt tight against his shoulder, aims, and then fires five shots in succession.

"Press the button, Georgie Boy, I bet you'll find that there should be a few holes in the target this time," he says, tilting his head to the side and pushes his bottom lip forward smugly, as he waits for the paper target to return.

The target returns and Georgina grabs it and bends over laughing. "You only got one," as she looks up at him, still bent over laughing, "And it's not even in any of the circles. It hit the corner of the sheet." She laughs even more, and then Adam slowly sees the funny side. He then begins to laugh too.

"I need more practice, how long can you stay here, Georgie boy?"

"I could stay for about another hour, but when did I become Georgie boy?"

"Why, has no one ever called you Georgie boy at high school?"

"No, why do they?"

"Yea, I'm sorry, I thought you knew that, everyone's got a nickname there."

"I know most people do, but I never heard yours, Adam boy," she says aggressively.

"I don't have one, but Adam boy sounds good," he says as he smiles at her.

"Well, thanks for telling me my nickname, but I have to say, I like it."

They shoot for over half an hour, then Adam turns off the music and they both go back into the underground room. They begin to examine more of the guns on display.

Adam tells Georgina that she should take one of them and hide it in her basement.

Georgina would love to take one of them, but she would have to find a good hiding place, some place her father would not find it.

"Take one of them, Georgie. You'd never know when you might need it."

"I don't know, Adam. Your father will notice it missing, or will he?"

"You must be kidding; you could take a hundred of them and I don't think he still would notice anything missing."

"Have you any place you can hide it?"

"Yea, there's one place in the boiler room between the floor joists, were I could slide it into the ceiling above the kitchen, no one will ever look there."

"I'll get some black garbage bags. There are a few of them behind the bar. We can wrap it up in them. By the way, you do want the Ruger or is there any other weapon that you would like instead?"

"I can't make up my mind. I like the Colt 45, and it would be easier to carry."

"Take both of them, and take some ammo for both."

They then wrap the Ruger in the black plastic bags and Adam puts the Colt behind his back in the hip band of his trousers. They then close down the doors into the underground room and leave everything as it is.

As they walk back to Georgina's home, they meet two cops on foot patrol. Georgina is carrying the rifle and now feels nervous as they walk towards the cops, but they just pass each other as if they didn't exist.

"Gee, that was close. The cops didn't even look at us, now I've got to get into the basement. I hope my father isn't home yet, I can't see his van. No, he's not here."

"Are you sure you've got a good hiding place down there? If you were caught with these guns, they could trace it back to my pop."

"Yea, I'm sure. Here, hold it until I get the door open."

They walk into the basement and then into the boiler room. Her father hasn't finished sheeting the ceiling in the boiler room and there are spaces between the floor joists that lead out over the kitchen area. Georgina takes a stepladder that is standing against the wall in the boiler room. She opens it out, then climbs up and tells Adam to hand her the rifle.

She pushes the rifle that is wrapped in black garbage liner at arm's length between the joists over the kitchen. Adam then

102

hands her the Colt 45 and the ammo that is in another bag; she repeats the process so that both weapons are side by side.

To make sure they can't be seen, she asks Adam to climb up and give his opinion.

Georgina remains on the ladder as he climbs up beside her. He looks up and then shakes his head as if to say he could not see them. The ladder is a bit shaky with both of them up on it, so they both climb down quickly having a good laugh as they do so.

"Do you think anyone will look there, Georgie?"

"No. There's no need to, but I would need to move them if my father ever decided to finish the ceiling there or else, I would need to break the ceiling to get them out."

"You'd better hope he never finishes it then."

"I hope so."

"Do you want something to eat? You must be hungry, and my aunt will have dinner ready for me and my dad at seven," Georgina asks.

"No, I'm going to have pizza on the way back, but thanks for the offer; I'd better get going."

"You can stay a little longer if you want, you must be lonely over there on your own."

"No, I'm OK. I might meet up with my gang members later. Would you like to join us? We would like someone like you on our side."

"No, thanks, you should get out of it; it's just too dangerous."

"There's safety in numbers, have you ever heard that expression?"

"Yeah, what do you all do together anyway?"

"We just hang out together. There are two older gangs around here that are into selling drugs. Some of my gang do drugs but we don't sell them."

"Have you ever tried them?"

"Sure, I've tried them; you should try everything once."

"I don't agree with that. I mean, what if you get hooked, and I hope you don't want to look like some of the junkies that walk the streets here."

"What about drinking alcohol? The Irish like to drink. Believe me, I've seen a few Irish guys coming out of that Poteen bar; they are usually falling around, shouting and singing. You must admit you've seen them yourself."

"Yeah, I guess you're right about that, but drugs seem to be more addictive and they're illegal."

"That gun you have in your ceiling is illegal but that didn't stop you taking it," Adam says grinning, in a ploy to get the better of Georgina in the argument.

Georgina just smiles as she realises the consequences of having an illegal weapon; lost for words, she shakes her head.

"What's wrong, Georgie Boy, has the cat got your tongue? Come on, your secret is safe with me. Hey, I'd better get going."

"Adam, thanks for showing me the shooting chamber. I don't know why I took the guns here. I can't explain why I want them, and I'll probably never use any of them."

"I hope you never need to use them either. I'll see you in class on Monday."

Georgina spends the rest of that evening in Susan's apartment waiting for her father to return home. She has a guilty secret and begins to think about the consequences if her father finds the weapons in the basement and what excuse she could use if he confronted her. Pat arrives home late that night and eats the meal that Susan had prepared earlier that evening. Pat wanted to get the Irish newspapers and asks Georgina to go for a walk to the Poteen bar. So he and Georgina make their way there. They meet a group of youths who are pushing and shoving each other. One of them, a young guy, about fifteen years old, climbs up on the roof of a parked car, then jumps on to the ground. He eyeballs Georgina and makes a crude remark towards her as she and her father pass him by. Georgina was incensed by this as she walked on, then grits her teeth and stops. Before her father knew it, she turns in a fit of rage, runs towards the young guy and grabs him by the collar of his shirt. The young guy is so shocked by this, he begins to shake and say sorry. Pat runs towards them, telling Georgina to stop. Georgina asks the young man aggressively, who the fuck he thought he was. Pat tries to separate them, but Georgina's grip only tightens. He repeats over and over for her to stop. Georgina in tunnel vision doesn't hear his pleas, turns to the group, and tells them to fuck off, as she skirmishes around them individually; they all cower. They had never been confronted by a single individual that was so enraged before. Georgina was a strongly built girl and even though she was only fourteen, she was five foot ten tall. Pat grabs Georgina by her arm and pulls her back from the group. She still shouts at the group telling them to get lost. None of them make any more comments and begin to walk away with their heads turned, looking back towards Georgina.

"What's wrong with you? You could end up getting killed doing something stupid like that," Pat says angrily and shaking in fear and from the unexpected reaction that was totally out of character for Georgina. "Tell me why you did that, please?"

"I'm sorry."

"What?"

"I'm sorry."

"But why? I have never seen you as crazy as I did tonight. I never heard you curse before either. It was downright dangerous; I'm fuming with you."

"I said I was sorry, Dad. I don't know why I lost it. You heard what he said to us, and I just didn't want him to get away with it."

"Next time, let them get away with it. Remember the old saying, 'sticks and stones can break our bones, but words will never hurt us'. Just remember that saying the next time some jerk in the street insults you…"

"I will; it won't happen again."

They walk another few steps, and then Pat stops to apologise for shouting at Georgina. She smiles and wraps her arms in a tight hug and is relieved that they have made up.

They arrive at the Poteen and Little Mick is standing at the doorway.

"Well, hi there, long time no see, Georgie," Mick says, "I haven't seen you in six months. Where have you been hiding?"

"I've been busy at school; we get a lot of homework."

"You've grown a lot since I last saw you, and you have a few more years before you stop. Pat, your daughter is catching up with you. She will soon be looking down at her little pop, isn't that right, Georgie?"

"All I can say is she will always be my wee girl no matter how tall she gets."

"Come in and I'll get you your papers. Pat, look at the new sign I got for the Mount Errigal Room; everyone loves it."

Pat and Georgina stand at the entrance to the basement party room and look at the new sign above the steps. They are both proud of the fact that it was down to them what it was named. They then buy the Donegal paper and make their way home.

That night, as they lay in their separate rooms, Georgina reflects on the night she would rather forget. She realises that she was wrong to lose her temper and that she would need to have better control of it in the future, if the same situation would ever happen again. She is also feeling guilty about the fact that she has guns hidden in the ceiling, and what her father would think of her if he were to find out.

But she also thinks about Adam, and how much he trusted her; she felt good about that. Her mind wanders to how Adam had shown her the secret shooting chamber. It felt like she had dreamt the whole thing up, but it wasn't a dream and she really was there; it was so unreal. She asked herself in her mind, "Was I really shooting a rifle today, I bloody was, I can't believe I did that." She hopes that she will be able to return there again, and thinks about her future, about her and Adam joining the army. She thought, by joining, she would be using guns for a living; what an adventure her life could be. Pat, sitting in his bed in the other room reading the Donegal paper, thinks about how Georgina scared him by her outburst of anger. He had never seen this side of her and it troubles him to think of what she might become. As he reads through the paper, he sees a picture of a few girls who attend a convent school in Letterkenny. If they had never left home, Georgina may have attended the same school. Pat dwells on this thought, but realises that he and Georgina have enjoyed every moment of their time in New York, also the fact that she would have more work opportunities when she leaves school.

Pat had begun building the new church in Far Rockaway. He was now employing three men to do the first phase of the building. They began by building small sleeper walls on their first week there. On the second week, two pre-fabricated buildings were erected fifteen feet apart on the small sleeper walls.

None of the men felt safe there as they seemed to be the only white guys in the area. Outside the gates of the site, drug addicts would smoke their crack pipes openly. They were harassed daily by young groups of men demanding money from them. After the third week, Pat decided that he would no longer take the van because he had found marks on the driver door, as if someone tried to break into it. Every night, material would go missing, so they would only have enough material delivered that they could use in one day.

Pat could never understand the fact that there were no visible signs of cops patrolling the area. He felt the good citizens of the area were left to defend themselves. They took the bus to the job every day and would hide their tools in the floor overnight by lifting a sheet of ply and then screwing it down again.

After seven weeks, they had finished joining the two prefabs together, turning one prefab into a worship hall, the other into two classrooms, with toilets and washrooms.

They had regular visits from the church minister who paid Pat by cheque every week.

The minister wanted Pat to raze the floor area around the upper part of the worship room and had a large plastic baptismal pool delivered to the building. Pat would have to cut a large hole in the razed area in the floor and then fit the pool into it.

He remembered being shown a house that they used as a church. They had a bathtub in the hallway as their baptism pool, and he was amused by this.

After two months, the church was almost finished, and Pat had completed his contract.

The electrics and plumbing were being carried out by two separate companies from the city. Men working for these companies also expressed that they had been intimidated by gangs from the local area that were trying to extort money from them on other jobs they had carried out in Far Rockaway.

Pat had been relatively lucky so far. He only had little material stolen, and a few minor threats made by local youths in the area.

On Pat's last day on the job, Georgina goes down to help him clean up the inside of the building. As they sweep one of the classrooms, they hear the electrician argue with someone in the main worship hall.

"You need to give me a donation," a man says.

"My boss gave you guys money last week, that was supposed to be the end of it," says the electrician.

"I'll check out your story, and I'll be back later," the man says.

Pat whispers to Georgina and tells her to stay quiet, but then the door opens and a tall, black male stands in the doorway. He stands there looking at both of them. He seems to have a small microphone and earphone on his head.

"I'm looking for a donation," he asks.

"I'm sorry but myself and my father are members of the church and we decided to come down here to clean up the mess left by the contractors. Here, I've got two dollars I can give you," Georgina says, convincingly holding her hand out with two dollars in it.

The man stands there and laughs shaking his head,

"No, keep your two dollars. I can see you two guys are hardworking people. Have a nice day," he says, shaking hands with both of them before he leaves the room.

They just stand there looking at each other smiling, surprised that he had fallen for Georgina's false story. They listen as his footsteps head towards the front door, then there is a loud bang as the door is closed. The electrician then comes in and asks where he had gone. Pat points towards the window. So all three of them look out to see where he went. They can see him talk into the small microphone that is attached to an earpiece before he begins walking up the street.

"Who was that guy?" Pat asks the electrician.

"He's one of the enforcers from a local black gang in Rockaway. You don't work around here without paying protection money," the electrician replies.

"This is my last few days working here. I hope I can get away without paying them bastards one red cent," Pat says.

"I overheard your girl here telling that guy some porkies about working for the church; you did great. Put it there, girl," the electrician says, smiling holding his hand up for a high five from Georgina.

"Yea, I'm either a great bullshitter or that guy is a fool," Georgina tells the electrician.

"Hey, look outside. The plumbers have just arrived. I'd better tell them about that gang, in case they turn up again," Pat tells the electrician before he goes outside to warn the plumbers about the gang member that was looking for protection money.

The plumbing contractor had taken five of his men there that day to hand dig a track from the roadside and take a new water supply into the building. He also had a mechanical digger on standby.

Pat and Georgina decide that they would finish early that day, but just as they are preparing to leave, the electrician runs to the front door and locks it.

He had heard a commotion outside and tells them that the plumbers are surrounded by a gang of men outside.

All three of them get down on the floor. They crawl on their hands and knees under the window in the main worship hall.

They peek out the window and see a black male standing up on the hood of the mechanical digger holding a baseball bat. A gang of about thirty men surround the five plumbers, all wearing yellow jackets.

The foreman leaves with one of the gang members, but the rest of the gang remain.

The gang member who had been in the building earlier walks up towards the door and begins to bang his fist on it, shouting, "Open up!"

The plumbers shout up to him that everyone has left and they had locked the building.

He walks towards the window, places his hands each side of his face and peers through it. Pat, Georgina and the electrician lie down just below the window hoping he couldn't see them. They can see his shadow on the floor, then after a minute he walks away to their relief.

When they look out again, they see the plumbing foreman return and watch as he hands a roll of cash to the guy that had been looking through the window earlier.

Within a few minutes, the gang begin to leave but two of them stay behind. They begin digging the track alongside the plumbers, but after about ten minutes, they drop their shovels and run off.

As they sit under the window, the electrician explains that the plumbing foreman was forced to employ two of the gang members as labourers; this gives the gang a legitimate reason for taking cash. As they hide under the window, they can hear a knock at the door.

"They're gone, it's safe now."

"That's the plumbing foreman," says the electrician.

"Well, as the shepherd says to his sheep, I'm getting the flock out of here," Pat says.

"Did it scare you, Dad?" Georgina asks.

"It did, but it scared me even more that you were here with me," he replies.

"I thought it was exciting," she says.

"Come on, Georgie, let's grab our tool bags and get the bus home," he says.

They walk towards the main street in Far Rockaway, then they take the bus home.

As Pat travels home, he glances over at Georgina on the seat next to him. He felt he had put her in a lot of danger taking her to such a bad area of New York and tells himself that it would be the last time he would do that.

They go for pizza in Jackson Heights before they head home.

Back in their apartment, Pat turns on the TV and sits in his new reclining chair.

"Do you want a cup of tea, Dad?" Georgina asks.

"Yeah, I would love a cup."

The phone rings.

"I'll get it, Georgie."

"Hello, Bosco."

Georgina looks as her father suddenly goes quiet; his expression of joy turns to dismay as he listens to Bosco, who is back in Donegal.

"Is everything OK, Dad?"

"Gran's been rushed to hospital in Letterkenny. Bosco says that she may have had a heart attack; here, you can talk to him."

Georgina takes the phone and Pat just sits in his chair in shock. Georgina talks to Bosco for a few minutes then puts down the phone.

As Pat looks at Georgina, she looks very upset; Pat stands up and gives her a tight hug. They decide to call Susan at the hospital; she tells them that she would arrange the flights home and that they should begin packing their bags.

At eleven that night, the phone rings again. Susan picks it up; this time it was her sister Mary who called. It was the news that they were dreading; Gran had passed away. Susan breaks down crying and hands the phone to Pat. He tells Mary to delay the burial as they are not sure if they would get a flight until the next day.

Gran's body was taken to be waked at her old home. Bosco and his father had been looking after it since Gran had moved out.

Sean Kelly picked them up from Dublin Airport the next evening as they travelled down the small road to the old home place that dark night. The lights of the cottage are on and a group of people are standing outside the front door.

After Sean parks the car, they make their way through friends and neighbours standing outside. As they walk inside, they are met by Bosco who leads them to Gran's bedroom where she lay in her casket.

All three of them begin to weep as they stand beside her coffin. Pat clutches Gran's cold stiff hands, then bends over and kisses her on her forehead. A few of his tears fall on to Gran's face. He goes to wipe them off when Georgina tells him to leave them. She tells him that Gran won't mind.

Mary then enters the room; they all embrace her. She tells them that Gran knew she hadn't long left and she says if she died, she wanted her death to be a celebration of her life, that she wanted no tears, and her final message was for Georgina that she was so proud of her and that she would always be with her. Georgina begins to cry uncontrollably. Pat holds her in his arms, her face against his chest with his chin resting on her head. Susan pats her on the back and tells her, "Remember, Georgie, Gran wants no tears." Georgina lifts her head up, looks at Susan and smiles. "That's more like it; come out and we'll have a wee cup of tea."

"Pat, I've got a bottle in the car," Sean Kelly tells Pat. "I've been saving it for a special occasion."

"I hope it's what I think it is," Pat then whispers, "Poteen,"

"That's right; it comes from a good source."

"Well, me mother wanted us to celebrate her life, I certainly will do that tonight."

Sean takes in the bottle of poteen and pours him a pint glass of it.

Georgina goes to her old bedroom. Her aunt Mary had left her bed ready for her and had a hot water bottle filled, which had gone cold.

It felt strange to be back in her old room after almost seven years.

It still had the blue curtains, although the sun had bleached them slightly.

As she lies in her bed with the lights off, she can hear people telling stories about all the good old days in the glen. This gave her great comfort, as there was a lot of laughter; it kept her spirits up. She can also hear her father's voice; he seemed to be drunk and slurring his words. *Gran wouldn't approve*, she thought to herself, then slowly she drifts off to sleep.

Next day as everyone gathers outside the house, Pat puts on his new black suit. Georgina compliments him on how good he looks. She had never seen him in a suit before.

Gran's remains are taken to the local church. During the Mass, Father Gallagher tells the congregation that Mrs Boyle would sadly be missed, how good a Christian she was and how she had helped raise Georgina after her mother had passed away.

After her burial in the local cemetery behind the church, everyone is invited back for tea at the cottage. Pat sits in his old chair. He takes down one of his old pipes, and Bosco had bought him his favourite tobacco.

"Here, Bosco, fill this one up for yourself," Pat says, giving Bosco another one of his old pipes.

"Me mam will kill me if she catches me with that," he replies.

"It's a special occasion; go on, take it," Pat says. "Sean, can your son smoke my old pipe, I'm trying to teach him a few bad habits?"

"Agh, one pipeful won't kill him, but don't let your mother see you with it," Sean says.

Bosco sits opposite Pat at the fireplace puffing on the pipe, and then Georgina comes into the room and laughs at the sight of Bosco smoking.

"What are you two like," Georgina says laughing. "Dad, you are not a good example to your young nephew, are you?"

"He could be doing a lot worse; it's only a bit of fun."

"What's going on here, Bosco?" Mary shouts standing with her hands clutching each side of her waist, as if appearing out of nowhere.

Laughter spreads through the room full of people. "You're a naughty boy, Bosco," someone shouts in the background, causing even more laughter.

Susan, who had been having a nap in Georgina's bedroom, gets up to see what all the fuss is about. It felt like the good old days as she watches Pat and Mary slagging each other off, jeered on by some of the locals. Susan decides to intervene, but Sean Kelly tells her that she's going to spoil everyone's fun.

The day passed with joy and laughter. Talk of all the great times they had as children growing up. Georgina sat on a stool listening to conversations and all the pranks her father pulled on the family growing up.

That night after everyone had gone, Georgina told Pat that Bosco says that he was coming to New York as soon as he turned eighteen which was about seven months' time. He didn't want to talk about it as his mother didn't want him to go.

Pat tells Georgina that he can understand that, and he says that it will be his decision.

After a week, they arrive back in New York. Tom had finished the church while Pat had been away; he hadn't seen any of the gang that had been giving trouble in the area.

Pat Dolan who owned the bar in Woodside was looking for barmaids. Georgina asked her father could she work there. She had just finished high school and was waiting to fill in some time until she got her results. He was a bit hesitant to let her work in a bar full of drunks and the fact that she was only seventeen. In the end, Georgina seemed to be a girl who could hold her own, and he decided to let her have a go at it.

On her first night, a girl from Galway called Margaret Burton showed her the ropes.

She explained that every third drink was given free by the bar and that Dolan's bar was a sort of employment agency for the new Irish after they arrive in New York.

Pat Dolan also changed cheques on a Friday and Saturday night; this helped pull in the crowd. That Friday night, Georgina saw Mr Dolan in action. A cue formed at the door and went around in a U-shape to the other side of the bar where Mr Dolan sat at a table wearing a pair of black-rimmed glasses. As each person sat down with their cheque, he would look at it, and then he would pull out the cash from different places on his clothing. In his socks, he would keep rolls of hundred-dollar bills, then in his trouser pockets, he kept the fifty-dollar bills and the one-dollar bills in his back pockets. He would keep changing until he ran low on cash, then go to the basement to top up every now and then. This would usually last for about two hours. This impressed Georgina because the majority of the Irish were illegal immigrants and had no bank accounts. It was a real workman's bar. Most of the men went straight from work to the bar still wearing the clothes and boots they had worked in, most of them covered in dust and grime. A young guy who had been drinking at the bar nodded to Georgina then put up his hand and waved her over towards him.

"Sorry for bothering you, but I heard that I might be able to get a job if I asked the barmaid here. This is my second day in New York," the young man says.

"Well, this is my first night as a barmaid, I'll ask Margaret here, I'll get her for you."

Georgina asks Margaret to help the young man. Margaret asks him his name, and did he mind what kind of work he was prepared to do. The young man says he would be happy to get anything. Georgina watches as Margaret goes up to a group of Kerry men that were drinking at the bar. She has a quick conversation with them, and points to the young man looking for work. She waves to the young man to come up. Georgina, who was serving a drink, listens to one of the men who tells the young guy to get a pair of steel-toed boots and a pair of work gloves and to wait outside the bar on Monday at six o'clock that morning and that he would be picked up by a man in a van.

Georgina could not believe how much money she was making in tips, anything from two dollars right up to ten dollars from every customer that left; this encouraged her to be as friendly as possible with the customers. Mr Dolan had been keeping an eye on Georgina, was impressed by how well she was doing on her first night and noticed how well she got on with the customers.

Two guys begin to argue near the bar, Margaret spots the trouble and shouts over to them to stop or get out; within a minute, fists fly and both men end up pushing through the crowd knocking people over and spilling drink.

One of the men was knocked to the ground holding his hands over his face with the other guy standing over him shouting abuse.

"Out," Georgina stands in front of him with one arm pointing to the door.

"Fuck off," he snarls back at her.

Georgina stands in front of him staring directly into his face and says with venom, "Get out or I'll put you out on your back. I won't tell you again."

He stands there for a moment and looks around; with everyone staring at him, he knew he couldn't hit a girl, so he turns around and walks towards the door followed by Georgina. As she walks back in, a loud cheer is followed by clapping, Pat Dolan stands there clapping too. He walks towards her and smiles.

"You did good, young girl," Mr Dolan tells her.

"Thanks, should I have put him out?" she asks.

"If you didn't do it, I would have had to; the only difference is that you did a better job of it," he tells her. "Let's get this other guy out too."

As they take a better look at the other man, they notice that he may have a broken nose, so Mr Dolan decides to get him a taxi to take him to a hospital.

They work till four in the morning until the last customers leave.

Pat and Margaret congratulate her on her first night as a barmaid telling her that she has what it takes and that she could make a lot of money on tips. Mr Dolan pays for a taxi to take the two girls home.

Back at the apartment, Pat had been sitting up, waiting for Georgina to come home.

"What are you doing up so late?" Georgina asks Pat who was sitting watching TV.

"I was waiting to see if you got home safely. How was it, I mean your job?"

"Brilliant, I got on great, I also made over one hundred bucks in tips."

"My God, you're making more money than me, has Mr Dolan got any more work going?" Pat asks, kidding Georgina.

"I'll think you'll find that Mr Dolan only employs barmaids."

"All I can say is I'm so happy for you. There's a small fortune to be made up there. He gets all the young Irish; all they do is spend all their wages in that place."

They sit up until sunrise talking; Pat decides to take that day off, so they go back up to Woodside to the Blue Sky Diner for a full Irish breakfast.

That week, Georgina settled well into her new job. She was now earning more money than her father. She realised that she needed to be able to defend herself as most of the guys that drank in the bar could get rowdy after a few drinks and cause trouble, especially at weekends when they would drink all day long. She decided to join the Lost Battalion boxing club in Brooklyn. She trained alongside the guys in the club, also started doing weight lifting there. She would go there at least three times a week. Fitness became an obsession, and she saw her femininity as a weakness being in charge of tough Irish drinkers, so began to adopt a more masculine look over a period of time.

She began by having her long hair cut into a crew cut, and also started wearing army surplus clothing and boots, like a rebel without a cause. Georgina began to be known as a no-nonsense barmaid. This suited a lot of the drinkers as they could rely on her to stop trouble before it even started.

She keeps a notebook and pen in a side pocket in her combat trousers, which she would use to store phone numbers of the Irish contractors and of new arrivals that were looking for work.

Within six months, Georgina was a well-known figure among the Irish that lived in the Queens area. The old nickname that her friend Adam had given her began to stick. She was better known as Georgie boy than Georgina. She liked it herself, it suited her image.

Pat, on the other hand, would sometimes glance at Georgina when she wasn't looking. He couldn't believe the change in her in such a short time. He felt he had lost his little Irish girl and was afraid she could put herself in a lot of danger by portraying herself as an outwardly tough person as if to invite trouble.

Nevertheless, she didn't like the idea that her father was giving her advice on fashion, this coming from a man who thought he was trendy wearing polo neck jumpers when he was hitting the town.

The old lady who rented the upstairs of Susan's home decided that she would return to Ireland for good. Susan and Georgina helped her pack all her belongings, but she left all of her furniture to Susan. This would make it easier for her to rent it again.

After nine months working in Dolan's, one Saturday night, the bar packed full of customers, Margaret points Georgina to attend a young customer wearing a baseball cap at the opposite side of the bar. She explained that he was looking for work. Georgina walks up to the young man.

"Hi there, you're looking for work," Georgina asks the young man who glances his eyes up from under the peak of his cap.

"I am, there's not much work back in Donegal at the moment."

"Donegal? Wait a minute, take off that hat," she says, tilting her head sideways to get a better look at his face.

"Hello, Georgina," the guy says as he removes his cap smiling. "Do you not recognise me?"

"Bosco, when did you get here?" Georgina says, gushing excitement. Without waiting for his answer, she runs around from behind the bar, pushing through the tightly packed bar until she reaches Bosco. They both wrap their arms around each other in a tight embrace.

"I like your hair, it suits you," he says.

"When did you decide to grow yours? That's why I didn't recognise you," she replies.

"I probably haven't had it cut in over six months," he says.

"Surprise," Pat comes up behind Georgina, grabbing her by her shoulders.

"How long have you known about this?" she asks.

"Two weeks, we kept it as a surprise for you," he replies.

"It's the best surprise I ever had, and it's great to see you again."

"Hey, Georgina," Margaret shouts from behind the bar. "I don't like spoiling your fun, but I could do with some help here."

"OK, OK. Just give me a moment," she replies, "I'll talk to you later, Bosco, when it quietens down here."

Georgina gets back to serving the customers, while Pat explains to Bosco about the way of life for the Irish in New York.

Georgina would look over every now and then in their direction. She could barely believe that Bosco was here. She is so thrilled about it. She puts them up free drinks for most of the night.

After three that night, there is only a handful of customers left so she sits beside Bosco, talking about old times until closing time and helps Margaret lock up.

After taking a taxi home, they didn't want to disturb Susan so late at night, so Bosco decides to sleep on Pat's sofa.

That morning, Susan prepares a typical Irish breakfast of eggs, sausages, pudding and bacon. At eleven, she knocks on the basement door for ages, then a sleepy looking Georgina opens up and smiles. Her eyes squint as the strong sunlight shines on her face. She tells Susan to come in then turns on the light in the sitting area were Bosco lay still wearing the clothing he wore over from Ireland. As the two girls talk, he begins to wake up stretching his arms as he lifts his legs from the sofa and putting his feet on the floor.

"Good morning, ladies."

"Good morning," they reply.

"Have you a sore head, Bosco?" Susan asks smiling.

"It's thumping, O my God, I'm not well," he replies, his hands clutching his head.

"I've breakfast cooked for you upstairs in my place; I hope you're up for it," Susan says. "We'd better try and get your father up, Georgie, if we're going into the city today."

Georgina knocks on Pat's door. She asks him if he was awake, then waits but no reply.

As she opens the door, a loud snore is heard by all. She turns her head and looks at Susan and Bosco who laugh at her expression; she then smiles and shaking her head, tells them that is what she has had to put up with all her life. She then opens the curtains on the small windows that are high on the wall of the room.

This startles Pat, who sits up quickly and asks what's wrong, to which Georgina reminds him that they are to travel into the city to show Bosco the sights, and that Susan has breakfast ready.

Pat and Bosco struggle to eat their breakfast as they didn't want to upset Susan who went to a lot of effort preparing it but seem to feel better after they do.

Bosco enjoyed the trip on the subway into Manhattan; it was a big culture shock for him to see all the different nationalities as it was for Pat and Georgina when they first arrived.

They do the usual sightseeing trip that day, visiting Twin Towers, the Empire State Building and the Statue of Liberty. Bosco is totally in awe of the city and can't keep his eyes on the ground as he looks up at the tall skyscrapers. They take him to a good Italian pizzeria in Times Square where they sit near the window and watch the throng of people go by.

Bosco tells them that he thinks that he would find it difficult to find his way around on his own in such a big city, but Georgina reassures him how Manhattan is laid out in streets and avenues, and that after no time he would get the hang of it.

That Sunday night, they take him to the Poteen bar so Pat could pick up the Irish papers. They introduce him to Little Mick who puts them up a free drink in the bar.

Georgina shows him the Errigal Room; she seems proud while she explains she was given the honour of naming the party room. Bosco was impressed by everything he had seen that day, it was so different to the quiet life he had been living in Donegal, even the warm sunshine compared to the wet and windy weather he had left behind.

After a long day of walking and sightseeing, they are all ready to hit their pillows that night.

The next morning, Pat takes Bosco for his first day's work in Garden City. Pat was helping the Gallagher brothers to renovate a single-storey house, by taking off the roof and adding another storey to it.

Tom introduces Bosco to the men. Bosco tells them that he had never been that handy back at home, that his last job back in Donegal was working in a supermarket in Letterkenny but he was eager to learn. Pat gets him to start filling a skip they had hired for rubbish. The next day, they decide to try him on a chop saw cutting the two by fours timbers. This didn't work out that well as he only knew metric measurement and made a few mistakes as the men shouted the measurements to him when they were putting the walls together.

After his second week working, he realises that he would never make a good carpenter even though he got a lot of encouragement from Pat. He didn't like being a burden to the men so he asks Georgina if she could find him work through some of the contacts she had made in Dolan's Bar. Georgina contacted a good friend called Raymond Byrne who was a foreman for a demolition company in the city.

He tells her to have Bosco meet him at Dolan's on Monday morning, that he would be on a jackhammer taking down a reinforced wall in the basement of a new building in the city. That Monday morning, Bosco waits outside the bar. There were about another thirty men standing waiting there, some looking for casual labour. If they were lucky, they would get picked up that morning. As he stood there watching some of the men being picked up, a white minibus stops outside the bar and the driver, a balding man with a Kerry accent, shouts over, "Are you Bosco?" He's looking over at Bosco's direction.

Bosco waves over, then picks up a lunch bag he had left sitting at his feet and walks over to the bus. The man puts his hand out the window to shake hands, then introduces himself as Raymond Byrne then tells Bosco to sit up front so he could talk to him in private.

"Bosco, I'm going to give you a new name," Raymond says.

"Why?" Bosco asks.

"Well, if you want to work right away, you'll need a Union card, unless you have one already," Raymond replies.

"No, I don't," Bosco says, confused how this would work.

"Well, your new name is Donald O'Neil and you are now a member of the Concrete Union. Here is your Union card, just show this if you need to. They're fairly strict in the city, so keep this on you."

Raymond then starts to drive up Roosevelt Avenue. One of the men behind Bosco asks him what part of the old sod he was from. Bosco looks around, he sees the man take a drink from a Budweiser can.

"Donegal, where you from yourself?" Bosco asks.

"Belfast, I left it twenty years ago and I'm never going back," he replies with a grouchy tone in his voice, and then takes another slug of his beer.

"You're starting early," Bosco says referring to this drinking at seven in the morning.

"The hair of the dog that bit you," he replies.

"What's your name?" Bosco asks.

"Tommy Doherty from the Falls Road, Belfast." He then downs the last drop of his beer.

Raymond tells Bosco that he will be paired off with Tommy that day as he puts all the men working in teams of two.

Bosco and Tommy are put to work on two jackhammers breaking down a reinforced wall that was in the wrong place. Bosco was a fit guy and had no problem with the tough work he was doing. Tommy, on the other hand, was suffering from a hangover and was glad to have Bosco do most of the work. Bosco didn't mind this as he had a lot of respect for the older Irish. He knew they had lived a tough life in the construction industry. At dinner break, most of the men go straight to a bar having no food in their stomach, including Tommy. Bosco sits out at the back of the building in the strong sunlight eating the ham sandwiches that Susan had prepared for him. He washes them down with a cool bottle of coke he had bought in a local pizzeria.

After his break, Tommy comes back from the bar. He tells Bosco that he had his liquid lunch; to Bosco's surprise, Tommy worked even better than he did in the morning.

They finish up at three and head back to Woodside, all of the men going to Dolan's bar.

Bosco, not wanting to be the odd one out, goes in too. They are joined by a second team of men who worked for the same demolition company. Their foreman was known as Galway Jim. He was a tall large man, a man that you wouldn't mess with. He usually sat with Raymond never saying that much but watching closely the entire goings on around the bar. Bosco mixed well with all the men. He overheard one of the men talking in the group and instantly knew he was from Donegal. He introduces himself and told the man that he recognised his accent; the man was also from the glen, a village about four miles from Georgina's home. His name was Sean Mullen; he had left Ireland when he was fourteen years old when his parents emigrated over twenty years earlier. He still had a strong Donegal accent.

They had a lot in common and Sean was keen to find out how things had changed since he had left. Bosco was also curious to know how the two Irish foremen were able to have all the false identities and Union cards for all their men.

Sean, lowering the tone of his voice, explains that Raymond and Jim work for a Mafia-run firm in the city; the mob supply them with all the false Union cards and identity. The rest is easy, as there are a lot of illegal Irish looking for work. Bosco is shocked by this revelation but not surprised. He also tells him a story about one of the Irish foremen, who invited him to his stag night, and how the groom's family had travelled from Ireland to attend the wedding, but how the groom went missing the night of his stag; then a few days later, his body was found in a ditch near LaGuardia Airport. He had been beaten to death. Sean remarked that his family had unintentionally arrived for his funeral instead of his wedding. As they sit talking at the bar, Georgina arrives and walks in behind the bar.

"Hi, guys," Georgina says as she greets a few of the men on the upper side of the bar.

"Well, hello, Georgie boy, three bottles of bud there when you're ready," a customer shouts over to her.

"Coming up, guys," she replies as she opens the fridge under the cash register.

"We'll have two more down here, Miss Boyle," Bosco says, looking for Georgina's reaction.

"O my God, are you still here?" she replies, surprised to see Bosco in the bar as she knew that he had finished work four hours earlier.

"You two know each other?" Sean asks.

"We're cousins, can't you tell, he has inherited some of the good looks?" Georgina replies, smirking.

"I thought that God had broken the mould when he made you, Georgie," Sean remarks sarcastically.

"Well, thank fuck he did, would you like to see another one of me walking around?" she replies.

They burst out in laughter at her crude remark.

During the conversation, Bosco is in stiches of laughter as the banter continues between Sean and Georgina with Georgina always gaining the upper hand in the argument.

Georgina gets a call at the bar at nine o'clock that evening from Susan. She was worried when Bosco hadn't turned up for the dinner. Talking loudly, facing Bosco, she tells her that Bosco is sitting right in front of her in a slightly drunken state. Bosco just shakes his head and gets up from his stool. He tells Sean that he'd better go. Waving goodbye to Georgina, he leaves through the door.

He makes it back to Susan's home and Pat is sitting, watching the news in her apartment.

"You're late and you're filthy, you'd better get a shower before you eat," Susan says.

"I'm sorry about that, I went in for one beer with the boys and ended up staying," Bosco says.

"Don't worry about it, Bosco. I ended up doing the same thing myself. You soon grow out of it, after ten hangovers in a row," Pat says.

"You haven't grown out of it yet, Pat; I seem to remember a few days last week that you were late getting back," Susan says.

"Oh, I had to see a man about a dog," he replies with a cheeky wink.

"Yea, right you had," she replies.

Bosco tells them all about the work he was doing and how tough it can be. He also explains how a family that are linked with the Mafia are the owners of the demolition company. As Pat sits listening to Bosco, he was eager to find out who the Mafia family was.

"Bosco, what is the name of the family, or did you hear their name mentioned?" Pat asks.

"Yea, Sean, one of the guys that works with me says their name, I think it's Corbally," he replies, unsure if he pronounced the name correctly.

"Did you say Corbally?" Pat replies with a concerned tone in his voice.

"Yea that's it; I remember it now, it's Corbally," he replies.

Pat shakes his head from side to side. He then tells Bosco about his friend Joe who may have been murdered by two of the Corbally brothers, but it was never proven.

Bosco is taken aback by this revelation, but Pat tells him that the construction industry is a corrupt business, no matter what firm he had worked for over the years, there have always been known links to organised crime.

While Bosco has a shower, Susan raises her concern at the fact that he is working for a known criminal family, but Pat tells her everyone is, but some just don't know it.

In the weeks ahead, Bosco is a firm favourite among the demolition foremen, as he is a dependable worker who needs no guidance, using his own initiative to get work done.

During that time, different foremen he worked under would give him a different identity. On one of these occasions, he goes with Raymond to collect the wages at the Corbally offices. Bosco follows Raymond into the building then goes to the third floor.

They then walk a long corridor to the wage department and knock on the door.

As the door opens, a young dark-haired woman opens the door.

"Hi, Raymond, come in," she says with a big smile.

"Hi, Anna, you're looking as gorgeous as ever," Raymond says walking into the office, while Bosco stands outside it. "I have one of men with me today. His name is Donald; come in, Donald." Bosco forgets his fake name and just stands there. Raymond repeats it again, but Bosco still stands outside the office with his back to the door looking up the corridor. Raymond steps outside the door and says it again, but this time stands right in front of Bosco.

"Donald, you must be deaf after all that jackhammering; come in so I can introduce you to Anna," he says.

"Sorry, I was daydreaming," he says with a wink. He then walks into the office behind Raymond.

"Hi, nice to meet you," Anna says, still sitting at her desk extending her hand to Bosco.

"Hello, great to meet you," Bosco says, totally taken in by Anna's beauty.

"I'll be sending this man to collect the cheques next week Anna, I'm heading Upstate this week," Raymond says.

"That's fine; I'll be looking forward to meeting you again," she says looking into Bosco's eyes suggestively.

"Oh, me too," Bosco replies nervously.

"We'll go, see you, Anna."

"See you next week," Bosco says with a nervous smile.

Anna just smiles and nods her head, watching as Bosco closes the door behind him.

"I think she fancies you," Raymond says, punching Bosco lightly on the upper arm.

"She's beautiful," Bosco replies. "I wouldn't have a chance in hell with a girl like that.

"She's a cracker all right; I still think she fancies you," Raymond replies.

"I can only dream," Bosco says, smiling at Raymond.

They go back to Woodside and go to Dolan's Bar. Raymond hands out the wages to his men who had been waiting there for him. Bosco had become very good friends with Raymond and sits at the bar discussing the work in the week ahead as Bosco was going to be left in charge. Although Bosco didn't show it, he was so proud of the fact that he would be a foreman for a week and couldn't wait to get home and tell Susan.

After a few bottles of beer, he heads home on the subway. As he sits on the train on the way home, he stares at a poster of Frank Sinatra, on it is the slogan from one of his songs, *I did it my way*. Bosco sits there and thinks to himself that he could make something of his life here and daydreams about all the successful men he could become. Susan and Pat were painting the sitting room in her apartment that evening when Bosco arrived home. He sits on the sofa that was covered in a white drop cloth and tells them about being made temporary foreman for a week. Susan, painting the ceiling, is thrilled by the news, hops down from the stepladder and gives him a big hug. Pat was thrilled that his young nephew was showing good signs of leadership at the tender age of 19. Pat gives him advice on how to manage the men in the week ahead. Susan couldn't wait to call that night to tell Bosco's mum the news. She knew she would be so proud of him.

Georgina was also given a promotion. She was made manager of Dolan's Bar. She never intended to make it her full-time occupation as she always intended joining the military but failed the colour-blind test. This was devastating for her. It meant that she could never live the adventurous life she dreamed of. She and her good friend Adam would practice in the shooting galleries in Adam's father's basement, when they knew that he was in South America on business.

But on one of his trips, he became involved in a shootout and was killed. Adam was never told of the circumstances of his father's murder. When his body was returned for burial, Georgina was a great support for Adam in his time of need. In his father's will, he had left him over forty thousand dollars in a bank account and the house. This was a total shock to him. For six months after his father's death, he splurged on drugs and drink. Georgina became angry with his outrageous behaviour. She slowly won him around with her voice of reason and made him realise that he now had a lot to live for. They both discussed what he would do with all the guns in the basement. He was afraid that some of his father's close associates may know about the stash. Georgina advised him to go to the cops and tell them all about it. If he were to knowingly keep them, he could be arrested.

He agrees with Georgina and they decide to take a few of the guns for himself and hide them in Georgina's basement that evening when her father was out.

The next day, Adam calls the police and tells them that he had only found the secret chamber the night before and how his father had never let him into it while he was alive. That day, the house was surrounded with cops and FBI agents. It also made to the front pages of the New York Times and all the local New York TV stations.

Adam was held in custody for four days but was released without charge.

He didn't contact Georgina. He was afraid that his phone was tapped and that he was under surveillance. After a week, he decides one morning to drive over and see Georgina.

He knocks on the basement door and rings the doorbell a few times, then after a few minutes, he can hear Georgina unlock the door.

"Adam," she gasps as she peeks through the gap of the chained door and then quickly unchains it. "I've been so worried about you; you look like shite; are you OK?"

"Thanks, Georgie, you really know how to make a guy feel good about himself," he says smiling, then hugs Georgina.

"Sorry, but I'm a bit of a mess myself," Georgina says squinting through her sleepy eyes. "I was working in Dolan's until five this morning, come in."

"I've had a shit week; I haven't been sleeping that good," he tells her as he sits in Pat's armchair. "They didn't charge me with anything. I didn't want to contact you until I felt the coast was clear."

"Have they taken all the guns?" he asks.

"Did he believe you?" she asks.

"It wasn't easy, but I won them around in the end," he replies.

"My mom called me," Adam says out of the blue.

"Did you say your mom? I thought that she abandoned you as a child," a shocked Georgina asks.

"That's what my pop always told me," Adams says, then pauses with a lump in his throat, he then continues. "She told me that pop treated her badly after I was born, and he would beat her up regularly. One of the occasions, she ran off with me and stayed with relatives, but he managed to track her down. He told her he would have her killed and force her to leave New York without me. She then went to Miami where she settled down and married. She had two girls, and she wants me to go down to meet her and my two half-sisters."

"How do you feel; you must be so happy?" Georgina says at the unexpected news.

"I was blown away; I can't express how good I feel," he replies. "But I'm angry at how my pop lied to me. He lied to me about how my mom was a bad person." He then places his hands over his face, covering his eyes and weeps in silence.

Georgina says nothing and sits on the arm of the chair. She puts her arm around his head to comfort him.

"Thanks, Georgie; if I cried like that in front of some of my other friends, they would probably laugh at me," he says wiping his tears with the tips of his fingers.

"When were you thinking of leaving?" she asks.

"Now," he replies.

"Now, you mean right now?" she says in a shocked tone in her voice.

"Yea, right now and for near future," he replies. "I gotta get out of this town. I'm sorry for telling you like this. If I stay here any longer, I'll end up like some of my friends, dead or spending most of my life in prison."

"I'm gonna lose my best friend then," she says in a disappointed tone.

"You'll never lose me as a friend. Here, look, I got something to show you," he says, rolling up his sleeve to reveal a tattoo on his forearm, saying *Georgie boy* in bold black letters. "I got this to remind me of you." He then laughs as he holds it closer to her face.

"That looks good; I'll go out today and get *Adam* right up here," she says grabbing her arm above her elbow and then laughs.

"This is the keys to my house, if you could keep an eye on it for me while I'm gone, that way you could still use the shooting chamber. You could take over the guns you've hidden in your ceiling," he says.

"That could be tricky now. Dad closed up the ceiling in the boiler room a week ago, the only way to get them out would be to cut a hole in it," she says.

"Well, at least they're safe there; no one will ever realise that they're there," he says. "I'd better give you my new address in Miami and this is my mom's number. Call me if you ever need me," he says, handing Georgina a piece of paper.

"I'll try calling you in a few days to see if you made it." She then gives him a long hug. They both have tears in their eyes as they part and smile at each other.

Adam walks away and up the steps, telling each other bye, and then closes the door. Georgina cries even more as she runs to her bedroom and rolls up the blind. She watches him walking up the path towards his car, and then sees him drive off. This unexpected news was devastating for her. She lies in her bed and cries uncontrollably thinking about all the good times that they had together. She realises that she may never see him again. Georgina had never thought of Adam as boyfriend material until now, but realises that they had so much in common, that Adam seemed to treat her as a friend. She herself was always standoffish when in his company. He knew secretly that she did fancy him but never made any effort to show him her true feeling for him.

She pulls herself together and decides to go out and get Adam's name tattooed on her arm. She goes to a tattooist in Sunnyside and decides to get the Poisoned Glen tattooed on her other arm also. This is something her father always advised against, but she thought that he was a little bit old fashioned.

Bosco takes charge of his men that week. His first day, he was a little nervous giving orders to the men, and they didn't take him that seriously either, but slowly, he won them around. He couldn't wait to get down on Friday to collect the wages at the Corbally office so he could see Anna again. He even travels back to Susan's apartment so he could wash and look his best before he goes there.

He walks up the long corridor, then stands outside her office door, standing there feeling quite nervous, fixes his hair before he knocks on the door.

"Come in," Anna shouts.

"OK," Bosco says.

"Hi," he says as he enters the room.

"Hi there," she says smiling. "You're Donald, am I right?"

"Yea, I was with Raymond last week," he says; again, he had forgotten about his false name until she says it.

"I remember," she says. "Sit down, I'll get the wages, you'll have to sign for them.

"Oh, no problem," he replies; he then tries to spell the name in his head and tries to remember his false surname, which comes to him slowly. "Donald O' Neil," he says to himself.

She hands him a form to sign for collecting the wages, then hands him a pen.

He then quickly signs it and hands her back the form.

"What's your real name?" she says as she smiles. "Go on, I would like to know."

"Ah, I don't know if I can say it," he replies stuttering his words.

"Yes, you can. You are the third Donald O'Neil I've met in the past year, unless you can change your appearance and regrow your hair on a head that used to be bald," she giggles as she gets out the words.

"I didn't know that, I thought I was the only Donald to use this name," he says, slightly embarrassed that she knew he was using a false name. "My name is Bosco, Bosco Kelly from Donegal."

"Bosco, I've never met anyone with the name Bosco before. It's a cool name, I like it," she says nodding her head in approval.

"I was called after John Bosco. I think he was an Italian priest," he replies.

"Well, I come from an Italian family and Bosco means forest in Italian," she says and they both laugh at her meaning of the name.

"I'd better get back with the wages," Bosco says. "There are a lot of thirsty men waiting in Dolan's Bar. I'll hopefully see you next week again."

"Yeah, I'm looking forward to seeing you again too," she says.

"Bye," he says, as he slowly closes the door. He then stands there for a minute and can't help himself for what he is about to do. He knocks on the door again.

"Come in," she says. "Oh, did you forget something?" As Bosco's head appears through the partly opened door.

"Would you like to go out for a drink some time?" he says nervously.

"You don't waste any time do you, but yea I would love too," she says.

"How about tonight or whenever you like?" he says anxiously.

"Tonight is good. Maybe somewhere quiet."

"How about Clancy's Bar?" he says.

"Meet me there at nine," she replies.

"Don't worry, I'll be there," he says, smiling from ear to ear.

They both say bye to each other as Bosco slowly closes the door behind him. He can't believe his luck, that the most beautiful girl he has ever seen is going out on a date with him. He can't stop smiling to himself as he travels back on the subway.

Back in Dolan's, he hands out the wages and tells Georgina about his date but tells her to tell no one. He didn't want the guys at the bar to know anything about it in case they started slagging him at work. He doesn't stay too long at the bar and heads back to the apartment to get ready for the night ahead.

That night, Bosco takes a taxi into Manhattan and arrives at Clancy's Bar half an hour before nine. He finds a quiet corner there and sits patiently for Anna to arrive. He keeps looking at a clock that is behind the bar. Every minute seems like an hour to him, then it passes nine and no sign of Anna. He worries that she may have had second thoughts. At nine, he notices a very glamorous lady walk in. She stands looking around in the dimly lit room. Bosco for a moment doesn't recognise if it is her, until she looks in his direction. She sees him and waves with a smile; he waves back as she makes her way to his table.

"Wow, you look fabulous," Bosco says.

"I have to say, you clean up very well yourself," Anna says.

"What will you have to drink?" he asks.

"I'll have a glass of red wine, thank you," she replies.

Bosco goes to the bar and gets them both a drink. When he sits down again, Anna wants to know more about him and why he came to America. As they sit talking, Bosco finds it hard to keep eye contact with Anna for more than a minute at a time.

"Hey, I'm over here," she says, referring to how Bosco is finding it difficult to keep eye contact.

"I'm sorry, I just find it so hard to look at you. You're just so beautiful, and I just get embarrassed."

"Stop it, I'll bet you've had to have a few beautiful girls on your arms in your time. Has anyone ever told you that you've got beautiful green eyes?" she says as she leans over the table with her chin perched on the back of her hand.

"No," he says.

"Well, you have, so keep looking at me," she says as they both laugh.

"Have you had a boyfriend lately, or have you still got one?" Bosco says smiling.

She hesitates for a moment before she answers him. "It's a long story; the guy I was going out with is in prison."

"What is he in prison for?" Bosco asks, shocked by her revelation.

"It's my boss; I never wanted to go out with him. It all happened when I applied for a vacancy as wage clerk in the demolition company. Giovanni Corbally was doing the interviews. When I walked into the room, he looked at me and says you got the job. We both laughed; he then had a look at my C.V. He then says you got the job if I agreed to go out for a drink that night. I know that he was a lot older than me but at the time, I was a little naïve and agreed to meet him that night. What I didn't know at the time was he was a mobster. I only found that out when I told my father about him. My father still fears for me. The other thing he had kept from me was that he was separated from his wife and that he has two sons. I tried to finish our relationship, but he threatened me, and more or less said that if he could not have me, no one could." She then begins to weep and takes out a tissue from her handbag. Bosco gets up and pulls his chair beside her, and they hug each other tightly. Bosco tells her about his childhood and how great it was growing up in the Poisoned Glen. She also shares stories about living in Queens and how protective her father is, but that he is heartbroken about her relationship with Giovanni and how she will have to end it.

Anna invites him back to her house in Maspeth. It is two streets from where she grew up. Bosco happily spends the night with her.

They manage to keep their relationship a secret from all Bosco's workmates. Anna also didn't want any of the staff in her office to find out. She was afraid that word of her new boyfriend could get back to Giovanni and there was the fact that she had not officially broken up with him in the first place.

Bosco began to look for a place of his own, one where he could take Anna without his aunt and uncle living under the one roof. On his way back from work, he spotted a sign on a house where the bottom floor was up for rent. It was four blocks from Susan's house. He wrote down the phone number and called to enquire about it. The Greek owner answered his call and lived on the top floor, so Bosco called in to have a look at it. He agreed to take it, a real bachelor pad with one-bedroom, small kitchen cum sitting room and shower room. He decided to move in that weekend. Susan gave it the woman's touch and gave it a good spring clean. Pat also did his bit and gave the bedroom a new lick of paint. This was the first time he had a place of his own, and he looked forward to Anna coming around to it.

Raymond, Bosco's old foreman who had returned from Ireland, was refused entry as he did not have a green card and was deported, leaving Bosco as a full-time foreman. He would meet with his demolition boss every Monday, a Vietnam veteran who would show him jobs that would have to be carried out by his team of men.

Bosco was totally dedicated to his job and planned his work carefully, but after a few weeks as a foreman, he had a lot of trouble with men not turning up on Mondays and would have to get his hands dirty again. He teams up with old Tommy Doherty from Belfast, jackhammering reinforced walls in a basement of a new building in mid-town Manhattan. Bosco was breaking down a wall with his jack when his right hand trapped between a concrete ledge and the handle of the jackhammer. He tries to pull it up but the chisel is stuck. He taps Tommy on the back, and because there is so much noise, Bosco points to the jackhammer thinking that Tommy would see his hand trapped, but Tommy misunderstands the situation and grabs the trigger on Bosco's Jackhammer, sinking the chisel deeper. Bosco roars with pain and shouts at Tommy to stop. Tommy realises what he has just done and tries in vain to pull it back up.

Blood runs down the wall from Bosco's trapped fingers. His face becomes pale; he is almost ready to faint. Tommy runs off to get a sledgehammer from the van as Bosco stands there unable to move. He gets back quickly with the sledge and beats the hammer back up out of the concrete releasing Bosco's hand. Bosco staggers away and sits down on a crate. Tommy apologises for what he has done but Bosco tells him it's OK.

They look at his hand and three of his fingers look to be in bad shape. He tells Tommy to get on with his work and that he would go to a pharmacy and get some bandages.

Bosco walks towards the rear of the site clutching the wrist of his bleeding hand.

"Piss on it," a worker shouts from a second story scaffold.

"What?" Bosco says, confused by the man's request.

"Yeah, piss on your hand," a second man shouts on the same scaffold. "It will sterilise your cuts."

"OK," he replies, nods and walks on with no intention of doing it, as the idea of peeing on his hand disgusted him.

He puts his hand into his pocket, as it was gaining him a lot of unwanted attention.

He makes way up the street until he finds a pharmacy and buys a few rolls of bandages, then makes his way back to the building site. His trousers around his pocket are now drenched in blood. He makes his way back to old Tommy.

"Are you all right there, man?" Tommy asks Bosco in his strong Belfast accent.

"I'm in fuckin agony, but not as bad as I was when it happened; I almost fainted."

"Your face was as white as a sheet. What kind of silly bastard were you, getting your hand stuck under the handle like that?" Tommy says.

"I'm not going to get much sympathy from you, you old bastard. Here, can you wrap up my hand?" Bosco asks.

"Jesus, you'll need to go to a doctor with that," Tommy says as he wraps up Bosco's hand.

"I'll be all right; I'll get my aunt the nurse to look at it tonight."

"Get you home young man; I'll look after things here," Tommy says.

"I'll be OK."

"Ah, cop yourself on; get the fuck out of here before I hit you a slap," Tommy snarls back.

Bosco takes his advice and leaves Tommy in charge, then makes his way to the subway. On the way home, his face was etched in agony as his hand seemed to get more painful. Back at Susan's apartment, he takes off the bandage and washes the blood from his hand. As he does, he can see that his ring finger and middle finger seem to be broken. That evening, Susan confirms his suspicions that both fingers are broken, and she makes two splints using lollypop sticks and wraps them in bandages.

That evening, he makes his way over to Anna's house.

"O my God, what happened to you?" Anna says as she meets him at her front door.

"I got into a fight with a jackhammer and the jackhammer won."

137

"I can see that; is it broken?" she asks.

"Two of my fingers are. I was hoping you can make it better," he says in a soppy voice.

"Come in and I will see what I can do," she also says in a soppy voice.

She makes coffee for him then tells him about a phone call she got from Giovanni earlier that day in her office.

"He is getting out in three months, and he wants to meet me again. He says I was all he can think about. I told him I didn't love him. He then started giving me hell down the phone line and says that he would make sure that no one else could ever have me. I began to cry, he then said he was sorry, that he didn't mean everything he said and begged me to give him another chance. I'm so afraid, and I think I love you Bosco, or I'd better rephrase that, I do love you," she says as she cries with her hands covering her face.

Bosco declares his love for her also and wraps his arms around her. He tries to comfort her. They both feel a hopeless despair as they contemplate their future, and how they could avoid the wrath of Giovanni.

Georgina worked in Dolan's almost every night but began to suffer severe headaches, especially early in the mornings, but they would fade during the day. It began to take its toll on her. On a few occasions, she had to take time off work and spend her days in the bedroom with the curtains closed as light seemed to make it worse. Through time, some headaches would last for two or three days in a row. Pat was concerned by the number of headaches she was getting because his father suffered headache before he died of a rare brain tumour. Susan booked her into the hospital where she worked to have a brain scan. It was an anxious wait for the results but after a few weeks, the news that came back wasn't good. She had developed a brain tumour and that she had only a slim chance of surviving the operation to remove it. Georgina took the news with grace and vowed to fight it. The hardest part for Georgina was how to tell her overprotective father. That evening, Susan and Georgina waited for Pat to arrive home, then at eight o'clock, Pat's van pulls into the driveway. Susan rushes to her door and calls Pat to come in as he was about to go down the basement steps. He then turns and walks towards Susan's apartment.

"Georgina's inside with me," she tells him quietly.

"Is everything OK?" he asks with concern.

"Come in," she says, looking him in the eyes.

"Is everything OK, Georgie?"

"Sit down, Pat," Susan tells him as she closes her door.

"I have some news, Dad; it's not good," she tells him as they both sit side by side on the sofa.

"What's wrong, is someone dead?"

"No," she says and smiles, then her expression changes to a more serious expression.

"She got her results, Pat, from the hospital today," Susan says.

"Dad," she then pauses for a moment. "There's no easy way to say this. I have a brain tumour," Georgina tells him in a strong firm voice.

"O my God," he blurts out, gripping the back of Georgina's hand. "My wee girl, I'm so sorry."

"Dad, I need you to be strong for me. I have a poor chance of surviving this."

"What do you mean, can't they remove it?"

"It's a 50/50 chance of surviving the operation," Susan tells him. "She is going in tomorrow. They are going to try and reduce the size of it with radiotherapy and chemotherapy, and she won't have this thick head of hair for much longer."

"I'm going to have it shaved off," Georgina says smiling. "I've always wanted a skinhead anyway."

"You're so young and so brave; I wish I could take your place," Pat says, his voice weak with emotion.

"The way I look at it, only I'm colour blind; I could have joined the army; like all combat soldiers, you put your life on the line every day like all them poor guys that are serving in Iraq war. I'm not afraid of dying; I suppose I'm more afraid of living," Georgina says, staring blankly. She then turns her head looking at her father's face; she can see he is in shock; she calmly turns around to face him and hugs him tightly.

Next morning, Georgina decides to go to a local barber and have all her hair shaved off. Susan had taken the day off to be with her. Unlike most girls, Georgina loved her new look and couldn't wait to show it off, but unfortunately, she had to go straight into hospital to remove as much of the tumour as possible. Two weeks after the operation, they begin a series of radiotherapy and chemotherapy. This took its toll on her; she became weak and very sick.

After her fifth week in hospital, she was beginning to find it hard to eat so she had a tube inserted in her stomach and was fed through it.

While in hospital, she began to have a lot of visitors from friends and family. Little Mick from the Poteen would go there every night to cheer her up. He had become one of her closest friends and she would confide in him all her personal problems.

During one of her chemo sessions, Pat and Little Mick sat at her bedside.

"Dad, did you know the only reason Mick comes in here is because no one else will listen to his bad jokes? He knows that I don't have much of a choice stuck in here."

"That's not true, Pat, she begs me to return night after night. I think it's because I'm such a handsome guy, well, so Georgie tells me anyway," Mick says.

"I'm keeping out of it," Pat says laughing and shaking his head.

"Give me your hands, you guys," Georgina says to Pat and Mick who are sitting each side of her bed. "I want you to promise me something very important," she says grasping each of their hands, then gasps in a deep breath.

"You name it, Georgie, I'll do it," Mick says.

"I'll do anything for you, Georgie," Pat says.

"If I don't make it through this," she then pauses, "bring me back to the Poisoned Glen. I mean I want my ashes spread over the top of Errigal Mountain."

The two men look at each other lost for words.

"Don't be talking like that Georgie, you're going to make it girl, don't you worry," Pat says.

"Yea, your pops is right, you're gonna make it," Mick says.

"Thanks for your encouragement, but I have to be realistic about this. I may not last another few weeks, time is not on my side," she smiles and looks into her father's eyes and says, "I'll be up there with Mum, my little brother and Gran, just you look after yourself, Dad, please," as she squeezes his hand.

Pat gazes into her eyes with tears appearing at the corner of each eye, then gets up from his seat and hugs her. He knows that no matter how much he wants her to survive that her chances are slim.

"Georgie, if you don't make it," Mick says, his voice etching towards a more serious tone, "I promise you, I'll make these tiny legs walk to the top of that mountain, and I'll spread your ashes on top. Is that OK with you, Pat?"

"I wouldn't be fit to climb it," Pat says. "You can have the honour."

"How long does it take to climb anyway?" he asks

"About two hours, but your tiny ass will probably take double that," Georgina says with a laugh.

"O, thanks a lot, nice to see she still insults me, but don't you worry I'll get there."

After six weeks, she returned home. The chemo had left her weak and very tired. She spent the next two months in her bed trying to recover. Gradually, she began recovering. After six months, she was almost back to normal. She began working in Dolan's again but after a month, she began to suffer headaches and nausea again. She had another MRI scan but to everyone's disappointment, the tumour had returned. Georgina's grievance with God became even greater. She now felt that he had targeted her and her family for no reason, none that she could justify. Other times, she began to question God's existence and this would make her feel even worse as she had no one to blame for her situation, only herself.

Her father took the news very badly. As they sat watching TV the evening she had received the results they talked about her having the treatment again. Pat did his best to cheer her up, but Georgina tells him that she feels it's a waste of time. She tells him that her cancer will not go away, and she has already accepted it. She tells him that we all have to die someday and that she is ready to die.

That night, Pat found it hard to sleep as he thought about Georgina. The little girl he had brought to New York had completely transformed into someone he could hardly recognise.

Growing up on the mean streets had hardened a shy and innocent Irish girl.

Her once long flowing hair had been replaced by a shaven head. Her pretty dresses replaced with combat trousers and boots. The more he thought about it, he realised that he wouldn't change a thing about her. She had character and everyone loved her for that. The fact that she seemed to accept her illness gave him some comfort.

She was booked to go back in for treatment on Monday which gave her three days of freedom before she went back. The thought of going back for more treatment was a cause of great depression for her; to take her mind off things, she decided to work at Dolan's until Saturday. She thought this would take her mind off her troubles and boost her self-esteem.

Bosco was made a permanent foreman with the demolition company, but his greatest fear was realised when one of the other foremen spotted him out in a restaurant in Manhattan, with Anna. He came over to their table and began poking fun about their relationship. Anna was afraid that news would get back to Giovanni, so from that night, they decided to only meet at Anna's house. But this was too late, as the news of their relationship began to spread within the demolition company.

Anna's worst fear came true, when Leo Corbally came to her office telling her that he had heard the rumour that she had been dating Bosco, which she denied and claimed that they were just good friends. Leo wasn't convinced and had told her that his brother wasn't too pleased when told the news. He advised her that she should end her relationship with Bosco and be prepared as his brother would be released within two weeks and wanted to continue his relationship with her.

That night, Bosco made his way to Anna's house. He wore a baseball cap and pulled his collar up around his lower face to try and disguise his appearance as much as possible. When he gets there and goes into her house using a key that she had given him, the house was in darkness from inside. Anna hears him coming in, rushes towards him and tells him to keep the light off.

"What's wrong?" he asks.

"I'm being watched," she says. "There are two guys that I recognise in a car. They are sitting across the street."

"Who are they?"

"They work for Leo; they are his enforcers as he likes to call them." "Shit, do they know about us?" he asks.

"Leo came to my office today and says he had heard a rumour, and asks me if it were true. I denied it, but he seemed to not believe me. I am so fucking afraid of these bastards. What can we do? I feel so trapped."

"The only thing we can do is to get out of this town," he says.

"I'll do anything to get away from him. They're making my life a misery."

"Where can we go?" he asks.

"No matter where we go, he will try and find us," she says.

"We've got to do it this week," he says.

"Giovanni is being released in two days. He says the first thing he wants to do is come and meet me. I can't bear the thought of seeing him again."

They look through a gap in the closed curtains, in the front sitting room window.

As cars pass by, their lights reflect on the faces of the men in the car, and they can be seen clearly watching Anna's house. Both Anna and Bosco couldn't sleep that night; they took turns keeping an eye on the car outside until morning. To make it look as if they didn't see the car outside, they both go to work as usual. As they pass the men in the car outside, they can see one of the men sleeping and the other keeping watch.

Bosco knows that the game is up and tells Anna as they walk towards the bus stop, that they should split temporarily until they decide where to go.

Bosco, who had been doing a demolition job with his team of men near Brooklyn Bridge, arrives to find Leo Corbally standing waiting with some of Bosco's men.

"Hi there, is everything OK?" Bosco asks.

"Hi, I'm Leo Corbally, I'm leaving Seamus in charge of things around here. Step outside with me for a moment."

"OK," Bosco says as he and Leo walk towards a back door exit.

"You listen to me," Leo says, grabbing Bosco by his throat and squeezing him until he begins choking and banging his head on the wall behind him, "If I see you near Anna's home again or if you phone her or even fucking look at her again, I will fucking kill you, do you understand me?"

"Yes," Bosco replies in a croaking voice, unable to get the words out properly as Leo is still squeezing his throat.

"Do you understand me, you fucking good-for-nothing Irish bastard?"

"Yes, yes, please let me go." Leo releases his grip, shoving Bosco one last time against the wall.

"And by the way, you're fired, you got that?" Leo says.

"Yea, OK," Bosco says, staggering away.

Bosco walks to the subway station in total shock, his mind delirious and his body trembling. He is finding it difficult to comprehend what he has got himself involved in and can see no way of resolving this situation and feels totally out of his depth.

Sitting on the train on the way home, he worries about Anna and hopes that she is not in danger. He prays in silence for Anna's safety, promising God that he would be a better person in return for Anna's protection.

Back in Jackson Heights, he goes to Georgina's apartment and knocks on her door.

"Hi, Georgie, can I come in?" he asks.

"Come in; come in, what's up?"

"O fuck, I just don't know where to start. I just lost my job and they know about me and Anna."

"Who knows?"

"The Corbally brothers; Leo Corbally almost strangled me today and warned me to stay away from Anna; we want to get out of this place, but we have nowhere to go."

"I've a friend in Florida; settle down man, I'll call him now."

"Thanks, Georgie."

Georgina calls Adam who is now living in Florida and asks for his help.

He tells her to get both Anna and Bosco on the next available flight. As Georgina turns her head around to tell Bosco the good news, before she speaks, she looks at him and sees how distressed he has become.

"Bosco, are you OK?"

"I'm worried about Anna. She's at their mercy and I feel helpless. I just don't know what to do."

"Don't you worry; if they do anything, I mean anything out of line, they'll have me to contend with."

"What do you mean?" he asks.

"I've got enough ammo and guns hidden in this apartment to take on the American Army."

"Where?" he asks.

"Just trust me, it's here," she replies.

Anna went to work as usual. She hoped that this would give the impression to Leo that everything was OK between herself and Giovanni. Later that day, Leo calls around to her office and tells her that he had fired Bosco.

He told her he knew that she had been seeing Bosco and advised her to avoid him from now on and how much his brother was looking forward to seeing her.

She bluffed that she was also looking forward to seeing him again and denied that Bosco meant anything to her, that he was only a fling.

Before he leaves, he warns her a final time not to let his brother down.

Anna worked that day but found it hard to function as she could not take her mind off how she and Bosco were to escape from the clutches of the Corbally brothers. She also dreaded the thought of Giovanni touching her and wished that she could avoid meeting him the next day.

That evening, as she made her way home on the train, Bosco was waiting patiently for her at her last stop. He tells her of his plan to stay with Georgina's friend in Florida, that it was their best option at short notice. She is willing to go anywhere as far away from Giovanni as possible. He advised her to pack and be ready to leave in a taxi with him the next day. They kiss each other goodbye as Bosco could not be seen again at Anna's house as it could still be under surveillance by some of Leo's cronies.

That night, Anna packs her belongings and calls her father that she is leaving the next day. She had never told him about her dating Bosco but her father never liked her seeing Giovanni anyway. He wished her good luck and told her to contact him when she gets to Florida.

That night, she packs her clothing into two suitcases and leaves them sitting by the door, ready to leave the next day.

Neither she nor Bosco could sleep that night, both thinking of each other and how different their lives will be from now on.

That morning, Pat and Susan call around to Bosco's apartment before they go off to their jobs. They feel sad but relieved that he has to leave so quickly, but as Pat only knew too well, Leo Corbally would kill him in a flash if he were to continue seeing Anna.

Bosco, who also had his bag sitting by his door, waits for the taxi to take him to Anna's; as he waits looking out his window, a black car parks outside on the street.

Two well-built men both wearing dark sunglasses and gloves get out of the car and walk towards Bosco's side door entrance.

Bosco instinctively knows that they are linked to the Corbally brothers and tries ringing Georgina. Georgina had already left to work in Dolan's, so as the men knock on his door, he frantically calls the Poteen Bar, hoping that he could tell Little Mick that he could alert Georgina that he may be in danger. Unfortunately, one of Mick's barmen answers the phone.

"Hello, Poteen Bar," Charley the barman says.

"Is that you, Mick?" Bosco asks frantically.

"No, it's Charley."

"Please get me Mick on the phone."

"He's not due in for another hour."

"O damn it, tell him I need help, that Bosco called."

"Why what's up?"

"I could end up dead; there's two men outside my door; tell him I need help," Bosco says as the door bursts open and one of the men walks towards him pointing a gun at his head. He kicks the phone from Bosco's hand and stands pointing the gun against his forehead.

The phone goes dead, and the barman just stands there stunned; he didn't know if someone was having him on; he also had no way of contacting little Mick.

Bosco is told to move back towards the kitchen and sit on a chair by the man holding the gun. As he walks towards the chair, the other man begins closing the blinds on the windows. He then leaves and goes out to the car. He takes out a large sports bag and returns to the house.

Bosco just sits quivering in fear. He is looking for any opportunity to run from the situation. The second man begins to open the bag and takes out two rolls of duct tape.

Then to Bosco's horror, he takes out a large knife and a claw hammer, then places them side by side on the table.

He then takes a rope out and begins tying Bosco to the chair he is sitting on.

Bosco pleads for them not to hurt him, that he would do anything they wanted. Then without any warning, the man holding the gun punches Bosco firmly in the face, almost breaking his nose. The man then tells him to shut the hell up, but Bosco is left dazed and confused after being hit so hard. The second man then takes the duct tape and wraps it around Bosco's mouth, feet and hands. When he finishes, he locks the door and turns on the TV. Both men sit watching it, saying nothing.

Bosco sits there full of dread, in a real-life nightmare, praying for a miracle.

Georgina, who began working at Dolan's again, mainly to keep her mind off her illness, had no idea of the danger that Bosco is in. She believed that he was well on his way to Florida.

She had often overheard comment about her appearance on many occasions and was in no mood for it that day, when three guys sitting drinking started picking on her.

"Oye baldy, another drink here," a small guy sitting in the middle says in a Galway accent; the other two laugh out loud.

"Have some manners, and I'll think about it," Georgina says walking by, not giving them any eye contact. Jim Dolan, who is walking around collecting glasses, overhears his comment.

"Ah, you lesbians have no sense of humour, get me another fucking drink," he shouts at her, but again she ignores him. "Are you fucking deaf bitch?"

Georgina is standing at the till with her back to him. Her cool exterior quickly changes to a furious rage. She turns around, reaches across to the man and grabs him by the collar of his denim jacket and pulls him over the bar in one swift move. She keeps her tight grip and holds him forehead to forehead, her teeth gritted, his body lying over the bar counter.

"Who the fuck do you think you are, you ignorant little bastard? Get the fuck out of this bar along with your two stupid fucking friends before I break every bone in your body," Georgina says with venom then pushes him with great force back across the counter. He falls backwards over his chair towards the floor, banging his head on it. His two pals get up from their seats and pick him up. They are stunned by her unexpected outburst.

"Get out," she shouts at them with one arm raised and her index figure pointing towards the door.

"You heard what the girl said," Pat Dolan says as he ushers them towards the door, other customers move out of their way as they walk towards the door. "You three are barred," Pat says.

"Don't worry; we won't be back in this dump," one of the men says sarcastically.

"Are you OK, Georgina?" one of the regular customers asks her as she stands closing her eyes and one of her hands covering her mouth.

"Yea, sorry about what just happened; please forgive me for my bad language," she replies.

"You did right, a taste of their own medicine," he replies.

"Good girl, Georgie, I heard what that little bastard said," Pat says as he walks behind the bar.

"If he ever comes in here or says anything to you again, I'll hit him myself."

"Pat, I should have just ignored him, I just lost it," she says almost in tears.

"No, she did right, Pat," the customer says as he sits listening. "That will teach him a lesson; some Irish come to this country and think they can do what they want."

"Don't be sorry, girl," Pat says. "This man is right; sometimes you have to teach these idiots a lesson, I can see it upset you; go on, you take the rest of the day off."

"Thanks, Pat, I think I will," she says then hugs Pat and leaves.

Back at her apartment, she sits on her bed, her mind tormented by the goings on of that day and the fact that she may have only weeks to live.

In her despair, she looks at a photo that she always kept by her bedside locker of her mother holding her as a baby. She tells herself that she will be with her soon but can't find a way of comforting her tormented mind.

The thought of suicide is a fast solution to all her problems; in the next second, she tries to convince herself that she will have to remain strong.

Leaving her bedroom, she looks up above the door leading to the boiler room, where her father had hung the Sacred Heart picture of Jesus. She prays to him, she felt worthless, that she had achieved nothing in her short life, and the fact that Bosco had to leave through intimidation made her angry.

Above her head, hidden in the ceiling, are the guns that she had hidden a few years earlier; because her father had closed the ceiling in the boiler room, she had no way of accessing them. She contemplates, if she had a gun in her hand, would she end it all?

As she looks in the corner of the room, an old baseball bat stands against the wall.

She takes it in her hand and looks again at the ceiling, if she were to break through it and take down one of the guns, there would be no turning back. She would end it all.

In her downward spiral of despair, she begins smashing through the ceiling, small pieces of plasterboard falling around her, tears flow knowing what she is about to do will be her final act, one of desperation.

Two plastic bags fall to the ground just missing her face. She then grabs a chair and searches for a third bag containing the ammunition. She then takes all three bags over to the table. She searches through each bag and places the contents neatly on the table.

She feels bad about the mess on the floor, so she gets a brush and shovel and begins cleaning it up. As she looks at the table, she decides which guns she will use to end her life; this was never her intention when she first brought them there.

She decides to write a note for her father; this wasn't easy for her. She knows how upset he will be but the fact that she is going to die anyway and he would have to watch her suffer makes her more determined to end it fast.

In the note, there is an apology for knocking a hole in the ceiling and that she wished to be cremated and her ashes to be spread over Errigal mountain.

She then loads a Ruger pistol and makes her way to the bathroom and closes the door. She sits in the bathtub with her back to the wall. She had heard that was a common way to commit suicide so that the clean-up would be made easy as all the blood would end up in the bath.

A sudden calm fills her heart. Her final prayer is that God will forgive her and that he would look after her father in her absence. She then places the pistol in her mouth at a 45-degree angle pointing upwards, this way she knows that the bullet will go through the middle of her brain; she then closes her lips around the chamber and taps against her teeth. With no hesitation, she braces herself and closes her eyes, finger on the trigger, seconds away from certain death.

The doorbell starts to ring and someone thumps a number of times on the outside door.

She releases her lips from around the chamber and breathes outward and quickly.

Taking another breath in again, she blames God for stopping her but wonders why someone is knocking as her father isn't due back for another hour. She decides to wait but the doorbell keeps on ringing. *Who could it be, there must be something wrong*, she thinks to herself and takes the chamber from her mouth.

She decides to investigate. As she opens the bathroom door, she can hear Little Mick's voice as he shouts her name through the letterbox. She places the gun on the table, then grabs a blanket that was covering the sofa and covers the guns that were placed all over the table.

"I'm coming," she shouts, and then opens the door.

"Sorry, Georgie, but I went to Dolan's looking for you and Old Pat says you'd be here."

"What's up, Mick?"

"Bosco called the Poteen earlier today and asked for me. Charley, my barman, took the call.

"He should be in Florida by now," she says.

"Charley says that when Bosco called, he said that two men were going to kill him and the phone went dead," Mick says.

"How long ago was that?" she asks.

"Maybe three, four hours ago," he replies.

"Fuck, who were they? I'll try ringing him," she says.

She calls his phone, no one answers for a few minutes, then someone lifts the phone on the other side but says nothing. Bosco, sitting tied up and his mouth taped up with duct tape, moans as he hopes that someone on the other side of the line can hear him.

The man puts down the phone fast and walks over to Bosco; he lifts his foot, plunging it into Bosco's chest, knocking him and the chair on his back. The man then walks around and kicks Bosco on the side of his face, knocking him out cold.

A minute later, Leo the butcher arrives; he walks in and the men lift Bosco up in his chair. Leo slaps him in the face a few times until he comes around.

"Hi, Bosco, were you and Anna thinking of leaving town?" Leo says smiling. "Now you're going to know first-hand why they call me Leo the butcher," he says, taking off his coat and rolling up the sleeves of his shirt. The three men laugh, a macabre situation that they seem to thrive on. Leo then lifts the hammer and looks straight into Bosco's eyes.

Like a lamb about to be slaughtered, Bosco winches in fear. He can't believe the nightmare situation he is in. He thinks of his family and how they would cope if they knew how he was about to die.

He grabs Bosco's hand and puts it on the table. One of the other men grab his other hand and pin it on the arm of the chair. Bosco moans, shaking his head, but this only adds to Leo's enjoyment. Leo then smashes down on Bosco's fingers a few times; even though tape covers his mouth, his cries are loud enough to be heard outside, so the third man walks behind him and places his hand tightly around his mouth, muting his cries.

"Now, Bosco, I'm going to give Anna a present from you," Leo snarls, his face inches from Bosco. "Your heart, I'm going to give her your fucking heart," he says laughing, reaching over to the table lifting a long knife as the other two men walk towards the two front windows, both peering through the slightly opened vertical blinds.

During that time, Georgina had pulled the cover off the table and revealed all her guns and ammo to Little Mick. She quickly lifts her suicide note, folds it up and puts it in a back

152

pocket. She tells Mick how she acquired them and how she never had any intention of using them. He tries to persuade her to call the cops, but she just shakes her head and begins loading a few clips, filling her combat trouser pockets full of ammo. She then screws on a silencer to her rifle and views through the scope, pointing it at the light switch on the wall. She walks to her bedroom and gets a balaclava that she had hidden in the bottom of a drawer and rolls it into a hat and puts it on her bald head.

"How far away is he?" Mick asks.

"Four blocks," she replies as she continues to fill her pockets with ammo.

"I'm going with you," he says.

"You don't have to," she replies.

"I want to, even if it kills me," he says.

"Did you ever use a gun before?" she asks with a smile.

"Sure, lots of times," he says in an unconvincing manner.

"Choose your weapon," she says.

"This one," pointing to a colt 45.

"OK, Clint Eastwood, take it," she says jokingly.

"Wow, what a beauty," he says pointing it across the room using both hands.

"It's loaded, be careful," she says. "Let's get going. We can walk there as it is dark and raining; it will be harder for anyone to see us arrive."

They both begin running back through side streets, Georgina having the rifle strapped over her shoulder, both hoping that they would meet no one along the way.

Mick asks Georgina to slow down as he is barely able to keep up with her.

As they approach the house, there is no one on the street; two cars are parked on the driveway. Georgina walks towards the front window, followed by Mick.

She looks through the small gaps in the blinds; she can see all three men in the room.

She watches as Leo rips open the front of Bosco's shirt, leaving him bare chested. She has to plan her attack quickly. She tells Mick to stand at the left window, she on the right window beside the door as she wanted to take out the two minders first.

She tells Mick to point his gun and aim for the back of the minder's head. This should be an easy enough target as the minder was sitting with his back only two feet from the window. She then prepares herself, leaning her rifle against the wall and taking aim with a pistol at the other minder. She then tells Mick he should fire first; she then would take out the second minder.

Mick, who had never fired a gun before, gets into a stance, his legs wide apart, takes aim, but then closes his eyes turning his head away from the gun by doing this, his aim moves slightly to the left but before Georgina had time to warn him, he fires, missing the man completely.

Because he took a wrong stance, he is thrown onto his back, the gun pointing to the sky.

Georgina fires two shots in quick succession taking out one of the men. She then kicks open the door, two hands on the gun, fires at the second man as he tried to get up from his seat, emptying the full clip into his body. Grabbing another clip and reloading, she marches up to Leo, the gun in her right-hand arm thrust forward, but Leo by now had gone behind Bosco, holding the knife to his throat. She stands there holding the gun to the middle of Leo's forehead.

Mick, who was slightly winded by his shot, gets up, walks with his gun thrust forward.

He looks over at the man whom he thought he had shot then at the other. He walks over beside Georgina with his gun aimed at Leo.

Leo can't comprehend his situation, his two top hit men killed by a girl and a dwarf.

"I got the bastard, Georgie," Mick says, convinced that he had shot his man.

"You did good, Mick," she tells him, keeping her eyes firmly on Leo.

"I don't know who you motherfuckers are, but you'd better put down that fucking gun, or I'll slit his throat," Leo snarls at Georgina.

She says nothing, just looks him in the eye. She then reaches into her breast pocket on her shirt with her left hand, pulling out a packet of chewing gum, and then with her lips, pulls one from the packet and begins chewing it. She looks down as Bosco holds his smashed bleeding hand. She then rips away the tape covering his mouth.

"Oh, thank you, Georgie," he then cries out. "He was going to cut my heart out."

"We were only kidding him on," Leo says.

"Yea, I'm sure you were," Georgina says.

"Put down the gun and I can have one hundred thousand dollars delivered here in the next ten minutes."

"Is that so?" Georgina says. "Money you have extorted from the hard-working families of this city to fund your lavish lifestyle, and you think you can buy me. I hate to think of how many people suffer at your hands. Little did I think when I first heard of Leo the butcher that I would become your executioner."

"What do you mean my executioner?" Leo asks.

"Like I said, your executioner; say hello to the devil for me?" she says, then fires a single shot through his forehead. His eyes roll back in his head; dropping to his knees, his chin rests on Bosco's as blood begins to pour from his head wound down his face. He then falls back behind Bosco with a thump.

Silence follows as Georgina gets down on her knees and hugs Bosco as tears of relief flow down his face. He keeps on thanking her for saving his life.

"We've got to get you to a doctor," she says, untying the ropes from around him.

"I'm not worried about me. They have Anna, I've got to help her," Bosco says.

"I'll take care of it," she says. "Find me the keys of one of their cars Mick."

"Georgie, it's too dangerous, just ring the cops," Bosco says in a concerned way.

"No cops; if these guys live, they will come straight after you. I'll take care of them my way."

"The keys are in the car nearest to the road, Georgie," Mick says. "I'm coming with you."

"No, I'll take care of it myself," she says, taking her folded up suicide note from her back pocket and handing it to Bosco. "Give this note to my father. Please don't look at it; it is for his eyes only."

"Just one thing before you go," Bosco asks. "Where the hell did you get the guns, and where did you learn to shoot like that? I can't believe what you've just done; you were like some kind of commando."

"I can't say; all I can say is it was somewhere close by," she says. "I've got to go, take care of yourself."

Georgina grabs her rifle and puts it in the back of the car. A few neighbours had begun coming on to the streets, most of them witnessing Georgina putting the rifle into the car. Mick hands her the Colt 45; he wishes her luck, and she drives off.

When she gets to Queens Boulevard, the traffic lights are red; getting impatient, she decides to floor it when she sees an opportunity. Half way across, her luck runs out, a car crashes into the passenger side, her body is flung forward, and her head smashes through the windscreen.

Minutes pass; she sits in her seat unconscious. She then can hear voices. Her vision returns and a black male is shouting and cursing at her. Looking around, she can see the mayhem, she tries starting the car and it starts.

"Turn the fucking ignition off, bitch," the black male, the owner of the other car, shouts in anger.

"Move back," Georgina says, pointing her pistol at his face, then begins driving off with pieces of glass falling into the car and onto her lap.

She races towards Anna's home; she is still dazed by the crash. Slowly, she turns in towards Anna's street and parks at the end of it, rain falling onto her lap through the broken windscreen as she sits there.

Looking over the roofs of the parked cars along the street, a streetlight reveals four men outside Anna's home. She takes the rifle and aims through the broken window, using the scope she adjusts it. She can see that all four men are standing under the canopy sheltering from the rain. As the raindrops drip down her face, a memory comes flooding back; she closes her eyes and she is transported back to the day she shot her first deer.

She remembers her anxiety and the fear she had felt before she had made the kill, then the sound of police sirens snap her from her memory as they seem to be getting closer, and it forces her to act quickly. She aims at one of the men and fires. She watches as the man grabs the side of his face, falling backwards against another man then to the ground. In the confusion, they don't hear the shot and pull out their weapons, looking around and seem to guess that it came from outside. She aims again and fires, a second man is hit on the shoulder; he drops down on all fours, then crawls and hides behind a parked car. A third man comes running up the street towards Georgina in a semi-crouched position. Georgina aims at him and at about thirty feet, she fires at him with a direct hit through his heart. In the darkness, the two remaining call out to him hiding behind a car. Using the cover of darkness, Georgina gets out and grabs the man she had just shot and bundles him into the driver seat of the car, she then puts her balaclava over his face and places the rifle out through the broken windscreen. She then gets into the passenger side and starts the car, putting it into drive; it moves off slowly as she steers it up towards Anna's house.

She gets out of the moving car and runs alongside it on the footpath using the parked cars as cover. One of the men gets up and aims at the driver. He shoots when he sees the rifle sticking out the windscreen, hitting the man in the balaclava a number of times. The car veers off to the right outside Anna's house, crashing into the side of another car and stopping. Both men approach the car, pointing their guns at the driver then one of them reaches in and pulls off the balaclava

"It's Elmo, it's fucking Elmo," he says shocked to see one of his men behind the wheel.

"Hi, boys," Georgina says, as she stands up from behind a car firing two shots at close range, killing both men. She intended taking no prisoners as she knew every one of her victims were a liability. With every chance, they would track down Bosco again.

Again, people look out their windows. Georgina rushes towards the door of Anna's house. She knows the cops will be there soon. Grabbing the handle, she opens the unlocked door; she then makes her way to the sitting room door and listens for a moment. She can hear a man's voice that seems to be talking to someone on a phone and the sound of a TV in the background. She guessed that whoever it was didn't know she was there. She opens the door quickly and rushes in fast, pointing the gun using both hands.

"Who the fuck are you?" Giovanni asks, holding his hands up, the phone still in one of them.

"Keep your hands up." As she rushes over taking a gun from a shoulder holster with her gun still aimed at his face.

"Who the fuck are you?" he asks; looking to her right, she sees Anna slumped over unconscious, with her arms stretched behind the back and hands tied to the back of a kitchen chair. Georgina can't see Anna's face as her long black hair is thrown forward, covering her face.

Georgina walks backwards towards Anna, keeping her gun aimed at Giovanni. With one hand, she pushes her unconscious body back into the chair then sweeps back hair from her face. Blood flows from her nose and lips and her eyes are swollen and purple in colour.

Bang, Georgina is hit by a bullet on her right arm, one shot by Giovanni by a gun he had hidden in the hip band of his trousers. Georgina falls on her back but before Giovanni fires again at her, she aims and fires, hitting him on his shoulder blade smashing through the bone. She takes another shot knocking the pistol from his hand. He falls to his knees, screaming in agony as Georgina gets to her feet walking towards him, then stands in front of him pointing her gun at his face.

Blood runs down her sleeve and drips from her clenched fist onto the floor.

"You must be Giovanni," she asks.

"Yes," he replies his face screwed up in pain. "Who the fuck are you, what do you want?"

"You can call me Georgie Boy," she says; the pain of the bullet wound was now a throbbing pain.

"You better watch yourself, Miss Georgie Boy. My brother will be here anytime now and he will have a bunch of guys with him. You won't get out of here alive, you fucking bitch. I'll do to you what I did to that whore on the chair."

"You'll do what?" Georgina says, banging her gun handle on his forehead in anger. "You scumbag piece of shit, terrorising a young innocent girl; you disgust me. You know my cousin Bosco came here to this country so full of life, finds a girl he loves, and she loves him. Then someone like you who can't handle rejection wants to kill them.

"Did you ever think that he had a mother who loved him? Well, did you?" Striking him again across his head with the handle of the gun.

"Stop it, stop it," he says, holding his hand up to try and protect his head.

A cop busts through the door and demands that Georgina drop her gun, followed by another cop.

"Shoot her, please, before she shoots me," Giovanni cries in the desperation.

"Drop the gun and put your hand up," the cop demands again.

This was the beginning of the end for Georgina. She looks into Giovanni's eyes then an old memory came flooding back from her childhood.

"You know, I remember something my old Gran said to me as a child," Georgina says with a smile as she reminisces. "She said that the eyes are a window to a person's soul. I really didn't understand what she meant by that until now," she looks Giovanni straight in the eyes.

"And you got eyes like a fucking cold-hearted shark. There's just not one morsel of regret for all the shit you've done."

"Drop the gun or I will shoot," the cop shouts as he and a fellow officer aim at her.

"You ain't got no soul," Georgina says, ignoring all the warnings from the cop. Giovanni smiles, believing Georgina will have to surrender her weapon.

"Good bye, Giovanni."

She then fires a single shot hitting him in the side of his forehead. This is followed by the cops firing three shots at Georgina; one of the shots was fatal, killing her outright.

Blood floods across the floor from her body.

One of the cops walks towards Georgina, his gun still aimed at her.

Both of them lie dead on the floor as the cops seek medical attention for Anna.

There was total mayhem as the trail of carnage that she had left behind was hard to explain. Her father and Susan were informed of her death later that night. They were both devastated and could not understand how she had acquired the guns, but during a visit to see Bosco, Bosco gave Pat the note in which she explained everything and why she wanted to end her life. Pat could understand why she wanted to do this as she was a very independent girl who would never have wanted to be a burden on family. This also explains why she did not want a slow drawn-out death. An investigation was launched to find out where she had accumulated all the weapons.

Both Anna and Bosco owed their lives to Georgina, to whom they were eternally grateful. They were given police protection as they were under threat from the Corbally family, but they didn't need it for long. The Corbally family had many enemies and a few of the other Mafia families were only to eager to take over their turf.

Georgina's body was waked in Woodside for two days. It was attended by all her customers from Dolan's. She was cremated as she requested. Little Mick, true to his word, travelled back to Donegal with Pat to carry out his promise, to climb Errigal and spread her ashes at the top. Susan stayed, and with help from Tom, organised the shipment of Pat and Georgina's belongings as Pat felt that he could no longer live in New York.

The word of how Georgina perished spread around the glen. Most of her old school friends found it hard to comprehend how she had died.

A Mass said for her was attended by Mick and Pat. Later that day, they both decided to climb the mountain together; both had a tough time getting to the top and had taken a flask of tea and a packed lunch.

It was a beautiful day as they sat and enjoyed the views, Pat telling stories about Georgina and some of the local characters of long ago. He also had a photo that he always carried with him, taken on Georgina's twelfth birthday, of himself and Georgina sitting at the top of the mountain. It was one that Bosco had taken and was always very special to him. They took it in turns to spread her ashes on the mountain and finished with a prayer. Both were overwhelmed knowing that they had fulfilled her wishes. Just before they descended the mountain, Pat had one last look around; he feels a certain amount of guilt, as if he was leaving her there all alone.

Mick stays in the cottage for a few days before returning to New York, but Pat vows never to return there; he felt, being close to the mountain, that he was close to Georgina.

One dark cold damp evening as Pat sat in his chair beside a blazing fire, puffing on his pipe, someone knocks hard on his door; he gets up and opens it and a small old lady stands there shivering and wet.

"Hello, I'm so sorry for bothering you but do you have a phone here?" she says in a strong New York accent.

"Sure, please come in," Pat says,

"Thanks. I need some medical help for my husband; he twisted his ankle on the way down from Errigal," she says.

"Where is he now?" Pat asks

"In the car," she replies.

"Take him inside first; I'll call the local doctor then," Pat says.

They both go out and help the old man inside and up beside the warm fire. The old couple were very wet but had a change of clothes in the car.

Pat calls the local doctor and makes a warm cup of tea as they sit and wait for him to arrive.

"Thank you so much; you are so kind; we are just so cold," the lady says sitting, drinking tea in front of the fire.

"Ah, no problem, I'm just so glad to be able to help you out," Pat replies.

"It's beautiful here," the man says with his injured foot resting on a stool as he sits opposite his wife beside the fire. "It's just how you would imagine an Irish cottage to look like."

"This place hasn't changed in one hundred years; there are a lot of happy memories here," Pat replies, smoking away on his pipe.

"We are so lucky to make it off the mountain before it got completely dark," the lady says. "Thank goodness for that girl; if she hadn't come along and helped us down, we could have died up there."

"You're very lucky, there aren't many people climbing the mountain at this time of the day," Pat replies.

"I know, she just came out of nowhere. We had been struggling down slowly after he went over on his ankle. I had just about given up and I didn't want to leave my husband on his own when this girl came down behind us and says could she help us, she said she was from New York also," the lady says.

"Thank God for her, she was so strong," the man says. "She almost carried me down."

"Did she say who she was?" Pat asks.

"Yeah, as soon as we got to our car, we thanked her," the lady says. "I then asked her name, which I thought was unusual, she said it was Georgie."

"Georgie," Pat says, as he glances up looking the old lady in the eyes.

"Yea, that's what she said. She then said she had to go and walked towards the mountain which I thought was so unusual as it was getting very dark at this stage," the old lady says; looking at Pat, she knew that he seems to be upset.

"Is everything OK?" the lady asks.

"Yea, what did she look like, this girl?" Pat says, his voice quivering.

"She was tall, had short cut hair, wore military style clothing and seemed to have a New York accent. She looked a real tough cookie, I can tell you," the old lady says.

Pat sits there, in disbelief, his eyes well up and tears flow down his face as he sits on his stool between the old couple.

"Did we say something to upset you?" the lady asks, getting up from her chair and patting him on his back.

"No, you've made me the happiest man in the world," Pat says, wiping his tears from his face.

"I'm just going outside for a moment, I hope you don't mind," he says with a smile.

"Go right ahead," the lady says, still patting him on his back.

Pat walks out and closes the door behind him; by this stage, the rain has stopped.

Standing in his front garden and looking towards the mountain, its dark outline against the grey dusky sky, he smiles.

"I know it was you, Georgie, welcome home."